THE FAR SIDE OF A KISS

Anne Haverty was born in Tipperary and now lives in
Dublin. Her highly acclaimed first novel, *One Day as a
Tiger*, won the Rooney Prize and was shortlisted for the
1997 Whitbread First Novel Award. Her first collection
of poetry, *The Beauty of the Moon*, was a Poetry Book
Society Recommendation in 1999.

Anne Haverty

THE FAR SIDE
OF A KISS

V

VINTAGE

Published by Vintage 2001

2 4 6 8 10 9 7 5 3 1

Copyright © Anne Haverty 2000

The right of Anne Haverty to be identified as the author
of this work has been asserted by her in accordance with
the Copyright, Designs and Patents Act, 1988

First published in Great Britain in 2000 by
Chatto & Windus

Vintage
Random House, 20 Vauxhall Bridge Road,
London SW1V 2SA

Random House Australia (Pty) Limited
20 Alfred Street, Milsons Point, Sydney
New South Wales 2061, Australia

Random House New Zealand Limited
18 Poland Road, Glenfield, Auckland 10,
New Zealand

Random House (Pty) Limited
Endulini, 5A Jubilee Road, Parktown 2193,
South Africa

The Random House Group Limited Reg. No. 954009
www.randomhouse.co.uk

A CIP catalogue record for this book
is available from the British Library

ISBN 0 09 928178 3

Printed and bound in Great Britain by
Bookmarque Limited, Croydon, Surrey

For A

So have I loitered my life away, reading books, looking at pictures, going to plays, hearing, thinking, writing on what pleased me best. I have wanted only one thing to make me happy, but wanting that have wanted everything.

WILLIAM HAZLITT

I

He has put me in a book. He had but a frail steel nib for his weapon but he has destroyed me by it as clean as if he used a blade and impaled me on its point. Let them all be happy now and ever to contemplate my vices – though I never knew before I had such. There was a time when he called me his queen and by other fancy titles – and next I am become no more than a juicy bone for him to throw to the scribblers in the newspapers for a right good chew.

To think that only so recent was I used to be Miss Walker, a good girl and daughter of a most respectable house – as we are yet indeed, paint us as he likes. And now am near as ruined as if I had my own gaudy couch to loll on in a bawdy-house under the rule of the likes of Mrs Hoskins at Drury Lane. And I have no defence, such as he has, open to me. Do I have famous men of letters to call my friends? There is no help to be expected from any of his. Indeed, they do say he has not a friend left to him in the world, as much on account of his headstrong character as what he writes – but any one remaining is hardly disposed to defend me at his expense.

Well, they always did think little of me. Now he has

given them good cause and they may sneer they were not mistaken.

As for his enemies, I dare say I might call on them. Excepting that I heard so much about them as I dressed his bed and blew his morning fire that I would not care to be the victim of their protection. Though I am now inclined indeed to believe that they may be the very best of gentlemen, for I have learned to my cost that Mr Hazlitt is never to be heeded again on any subject.

He has painted me in the most lurid wash. I am no better, according to him, than spoils for a common seducer. I cannot go about any more, even if Father was to let me. Low fellows would mutter at me from the shadows at the street corners and offer me ninepence to go off with them, believing me to be such as he said. And yet, he declared – for he is full of contradictions – that I did not know what doors and windows were, so devoted was I to the kitchen and the parlour. You are also therefore to consider me as retiring as a female of the Mohammedans who never leaves her patio.

Well, I am as well locked up behind the doors and windows now as if I were in Newgate or Coldbath Fields. And where could I go even if I was to venture out smothered in an Arab veil? Martha, who is the only friend I have left in the world, wails that she can claim no more to be a respectable lady, though by her own conduct she well deserves the title, as her sister is not. And I would hardly find my dear Henry at home had I the boldness now to go and knock.

I may as well take to the thieving of cabbages and be brought up before the magistrate at the Old Bailey and be transported for a punishment to Bottomless, where I might stray among the savages. Indeed I would not be surprised if they came for me anyway for the crime of debauchery. Why, they tried the Queen for the same offence, though she got off. It could be no help to me

2

to get off. I might die in my chains and find a watery grave and it would be no assistance to me, since my name has no means of dying along with the wretched frame that bears it.

What is a book? My brother Cajah, fed up with my weeping, begs me to ponder that question. 'Hazlitt's is a bad book, it will be fast forgotten,' he pronounces.

He is mistaken. For when there is even one copy of it about in the world, a book is less mortal than any being, though she live a hundred years. And here is one in which I shall live twice or five or ten times as long in the costume of a lewd and stony-hearted drab that he has dressed me in. I believe I should be glad to be brought up before the Assizes for a felon if I could tell it all. How it is he who is the thief, for he has robbed a girl's good name, which is of more value to her than any diamond necklace or fancy gig.

2

I think my father should take some little portion of my shame since it was he who agreed to accept Mr Hazlitt for a lodger. Father was happy to have him, having gone some time previous to see him give his lectures at the Institute and after that considered him a great man and of course he was a dissenter as my father was. Oh, we were all to consider it an honour indeed to sleep under the same roof as such a man as Mr Hazlitt.

My father may be only a tailor but he is a man of good character. While famous Mr Hazlitt, man of letters, professes to be good but is surely ten times worse than any. My father is not a man to know how Mr Hazlitt expected to be served kisses with his morning tea and was liable to preach that he was ill-used if he did not get them. One thing I am sorry for is that my father did not take me along to hear him at the Institute. I might have been able to love him then in the manner he hoped for as I was not yet used to lipping. If she is bad, he has made her so . . . That is what they claimed as an excuse to pardon the poor Queen Caroline. I dare say they are better disposed to excuse you if you are a queen. In any case, excused or no, she was dead within the year.

It was in the middle of the month of August in the

year 1820 when he came to us. I remember it so clear because I was absent from home – and would that I had remained so. At the time of his appearance I was stopping with the Roscoes in Dyer's Buildings to assist with the welcome into the world of my sister's first babe, who is Emma, my niece. I went there on the day of the eclipse, when the light of noon turned of an instant into the cool dusk of evening, and stayed two weeks. In consequence I missed the opportunity to welcome Mr Hazlitt in the grateful manner that I dare say my father would have wished. He got Mr Bradley's apartments, which were lying vacant since that gentleman quit them.

I was fonder of Mr Bradley than a girl in my position has a right to be and was given to melancholy fits after he left. Seeing as Martha and I were together a week, I found myself confiding to her much of what had passed between me and Mr Bradley. She was grieved at my conduct as she is herself so good, or at least believes herself to be, and gave me strong advice concerning my conduct in the future, such as, she said, a mother should give.

'I wish Mother were better in certain respects,' she sighed. By that she meant that she wished our mother were blessed with refinement and was not the old-fashioned body she is.

At my sister's I enjoyed a room all to myself fitted up with elegancies I do not have at home, in particular a green silk counterpane, and a pair of silver candlesticks with a snuffer to match that came down from the Roscoes' fine place in Liverpool. For a night or two at first I lay awake for a long hour, missing my little sister Betsy in the bed, and I missed her in the day too, for the new babe, though sweet, was not able to chatter as she does, and therefore I had too generous an opportunity to think on Mr Bradley. After that, I suppose when I could think up nothing further concerning him, I began to be more cheerful.

Old Mr Roscoe, who is a banker and a man of standing and is said to be highly esteemed in Liverpool, was also, and for the same reason that I was, a visitor to the house. His son gave a special dinner in his honour. We had two removes, several dishes of what my sister is pleased to call garden esculents – for the Roscoes, having Pythagorean tastes, are great for feeding on vegetables – and strawberry ices for our dessert. During this lengthy repast the old gentleman happened to observe me and offered the gallant remark that if his new granddaughter were to be half as pretty as her aunt, she would be well served.

'I am driven to regret, Robert,' he said, turning to his son, 'that you do not have a brother who might suit Miss Walker. I would be more than happy to further strengthen the connection between the two families.'

I flushed up. Martha flushed also, though in her case it was with pleasure, as she regarded the compliment to be directed towards herself as much as towards me. But my blush was one of embarrassment, as old Mr Roscoe takes every opportunity, by protesting his love for our family, to display his consciousness of how humble we are and his virtue in not holding it against us. That was the only form of sweethearting to be had at the Roscoes'.

Martha presented me with her striped muslin gown when I was taking my leave for Southampton Buildings, and two bonnets, though I am inclined to think this was because they were in the high-crowned style and quite gone out of fashion. But they were well enough for me. Old Mr Roscoe obliged his manservant, who he brought with him from Liverpool, to carry my box and himself kept me company on the short walk, though I believe since he is elderly and used to driving that he found it more than sufficient exercise for the day. He offered me no further gallantries but confined his conversation to remarking on the differences in size and quality and quantity between the buildings and people and so on of London and Liverpool, down to the very colour of the air. In most everything, he decided, London was the bigger but Liverpool was its superior. Arriving at Number 9, which is our house, he surveyed it with interest but made no comparison. He declined to come in when I suggested it, but tipped his hat to me very gracious as he went off.

At home, I found them all quite content, for they were busy over a great dish of oysters for supper which were just then come back in the market. The whole talk at table was of the sweetness and plumpness of a tender young oyster – for at home they do enjoy their victuals – and, second to that, the habits of the new lodger, Mr Hazlitt.

'He may be a great genius and dissenter enough to please your father,' my mother complained, 'but we are sure to lose money on his custom. He takes tea by the soup-dish and I will be obliged to send to Twining's every other day for black Bohea to fill his caddy if he continues.'

She would be better off, she grumbled, with a man who took strong drink in place of tea, as the mistress of a house is not obliged to supply her lodgers with their hollands or ale as she is their tea. It was plain, she said, that Mr Hazlitt was a man whose temperament was inclined natural to drink, and no doubt he would be yearning for it like an infant for its milk even though he refused it, and in consequence could prove hard to manage. But Father would have him. And I was not to tarry in the morning, and was not to go about in my morning-gown till noon but must put on my new gown that Martha was so kind as to give me, and be up sharp to light his fire and bring him his kettle and his tray. 'Though he bestirs himself late in the morning,' she said, 'and it will be an easy enough task for you, Sally.'

'Pray do not call me Sally any more,' I told her.

'What is wrong with Sally?'

'Martha says Sarah is to be preferred as a name for a young lady.'

'You may keep your notions, Sarah, I am sure,' Mother replied good-humoured, 'if it will bring you for a husband a gentleman as good as she has in Mr Roscoe.'

She wanted then to hear more of her granddaughter, though already I had told her as much as a babe who is only a few days old warrants. My little brother set up a noise in his corner, encouraging me to remark I had seen enough of my niece to know I should never wish to be burdened with the care of children, for they were as much a nuisance as ten Mr Hazlitts could ever be.

'You will never marry, then, Sal,' she declared.

I agreed I would not, for I was thinking of Mr Bradley.

'She will only ever marry Mr Bradley,' announced Betsy, who is far too quick at knowing my thoughts. 'She told me so. And since Mr Bradley does not wish to marry her, but went away and left her, she can never marry.'

Cajah then had to put in his spake and declared that on the contrary he had no doubt I would marry in a flash, for, he said, 'Sal is a kissing kind of girl.'

For that remark, I hove a crust of the loaf at him. And his shout caused my father to look up from his newspaper and to say he hoped I would kiss only a man I could esteem. I was cross to be the subject of advice and knew that what he meant was a man *he* could esteem. He did not much esteem Mr Bradley – being a man, he once remarked, who arranged his opinions to suit this fellow or that, whatever was to his advantage.

I was tired from all the prattling in my sister's house and now here it was in my own, only worse, not to speak of the wails of a newborn in one and a totterer in the other. I left them and went to my room to go on with my book, the *Life of William Penn*, lent me by Mr Roscoe. I wished to be able to give him my opinion of it, for he had remarked to my sister that I might be a clever girl were I not so dreamy and could apply my mind in a disciplined manner. I should read slow and careful and with the determination to comprehend what I read.

At that time I yet had a strong belief in the benefits of book-reading. After all, what I could observe of the world was limited, seeing as I was but a female. I considered it an advantage to avail myself of the ears and eyes of others who had seen and heard more of it than I ever would. I reached page twenty-one in Mr Roscoe's book. And that, I believe, was as far as ever I got with that particular work, for after this my reading-hours, such as they were, were consumed in the study of Mr Hazlitt's works.

3

I had been contented enough to come home. But on waking I was afflicted by the knowledge that I was no longer the young lady visiting at the Roscoes' but was to take up again the part of a lodging-house drudge. My sister may say there is all the difference in the world between the position of a drudge in a lodging-house and the daughter of it – but then, she has made good her escape from both. There was not half the toiling up and down the stairs at the Roscoes' even when I made myself some use to them. And yet I wonder now that I did not enjoy my work more and be grateful for it, even with all the lugging of pails and trays, when I had the benefit of a good character and an independent step.

The kitchen struck me as being pokier and darker and staler than I remembered. Lizzie was stooped over the fire, blowing up a great blaze, just when there was least need of it. In winter she is as liable to keep it low. In our kitchen you are either stewed or starved. My father was gone off to his shop, my mother in the street spouting to the dustman and Betsy running about the yard after Baby with his dish of gruel. Cajah was still abed. And I was back in the old grind of toasts and trays.

The Welshman on the first floor, Mr Griffith, assuring me he was glad to see me home again, pinched my cheek and admired my colour – though it had not changed I'm sure, while I was at the Roscoes'. He also admired Martha's dress I had put on. Then he went off to his dispensary with his apothecary's bag in one hand and a slice of greasy toast in the other, leaving me to loiter at my ease over the making up of his bed and the dusting, which had been much neglected while I was away. He can be quite careless and slovenly in his person, but Mr Griffith is liable to notice if his room is not dusted at the end of a week. And he cares a great deal that his bug-tray and his mousetrap are tended, for he has a horror of vermin, and cares too, like all the gentlemen, that his fire is kept well supplied – though there was no need for that just then.

At ten o'clock I prepared another breakfast-tray and carried it and a boiling kettle up to the top of the house. From the kitchen to the pair of red rooms which had been most lately Mr Bradley's there are four sets of stairs to be climbed. Is it to be wondered that a girl should want a little moment's rest after such a climb, especially if she is burdened with some necessary or other, as in general she is? Athough now that they were occupied by the new gentleman, who was Mr Hazlitt, I set about my work at once. I have to say I had little curiosity about him as I was sure he could be no improvement on Mr Bradley.

'Good morning, sir,' I said in a low voice on entering, for I am shy when I first face a new lodger. His reply was lower still and there was not a clear word you could make out in it. After that he remained silent, as did I, which is only natural. I thought him a morose fellow and, from a glance or two in his direction when he was not aware of it, found he had an appearance to match. He was a low-sized man and of an age not to enchant a girl. He seemed weighed down by the thick woollen morning-gown he was wrapped up in though there was no necessity for it, for the morning was heavy and sultry. I wondered that he was not gentleman enough to own a silk. He appeared to be hardly conscious of my presence and to be made no happier by it, only that he stepped out of my way to sit in the easy-chair by the empty grate so that I could move more easy about the room.

I was made melancholy and regretful of my lot from being in those rooms with a stranger in place of Mr Bradley and to be performing the same services for him in quite a bleaker atmosphere. It was only when I was quitting the room that I looked proper at Mr Hazlitt to see what kind of man it was who had taken my dear friend's place. It is true that I may have stared at him as he has written. But this was not out of the calculation which he imputes to me. It is a habit I have, my eyes not being sharp, and in consequence I am likely to stare at people without meaning to. If there was anything other than curiosity in my expression I am sure it was no more than a natural disappointment at seeing a stranger where I was used to see a friend. By dint of looking at him very closely I saw he returned my look. It impressed me as being of an alarming degree of intensity. Being a modest girl, and shy, I at once dropped my eyes and left him.

That was the first I saw of the great Mr Hazlitt. Well, I am obliged to say that I saw nothing extraordinary enough to mark him out as great. He had dark, unkempt hair with a little grey scattered in it. His complexion was passing pale, a consequence, I assumed, of the onerous gown he wore on a warm day and the volume of tea he was used to drink on account of his addiction that my mother spoke of, as well as his sedentary occupation. The eyes stood out sure enough, as they are said to do in men of genius, from his precise-fashioned face that seemed bonier than it might be.

Besides a good quantity of books, he had few personal articles dispersed about his apartments. There was hardly a thing on his dressing-table that we had not provided for him excepting his shaving-instrument. He had placed but one ornament on his mantelshelf, a little china figure of a man that I started at, for I was struck by the notion that it had a great look of Mr Bradley. My Mr Bradley was not half so rounded but he had a similar proud bearing.

My brother laughed at me when I was downstairs and was exclaiming at the likeness. 'Why, that little figure is no other than Boney. The great Napoleon Bonaparte who led the French to their Waterloo. And your Mr Bradley would have led you to yours Sal, if you were not so careful. Hazlitt keeps him like an idol on his shelf because he is an old Jack, despite everything, and will not give up his fondness for Boney even if the fellow is kept like a common felon on Saint Helena.'

I was not surprised to know the new lodger was an old Jacobin, as my father too saw something to admire in Napoleon now he was defeated, and they were near in age enough to have the same opinions.

The next morning when I was again in Mr Hazlitt's room, I found his writing-things were now laid out on his table next to the brown-stained teapot standing on its spirit lamp. I thought he could not be a poor man, as I saw he had a steel nib to his pen that was lying next to his foolscap. A steel nib is dear and hard come by; indeed, I am not sure I had seen one in use before as our gentlemen in general content themselves with a feather. Many of our gentlemen also have their foolscap and inkpots laid out. But Mr Hazlitt's showed uncommon industry as his table displayed a multitude of sheets with a well-formed scrawl covering them. I had the impression it was no great labour to him to fill the pages.

After I had brewed his tea and set it out it was natural

13

to expect that he would wish to sit down to his breakfast. I went into his chamber and fell to the dressing of his bed. In a little while I was aware that he had left off breakfasting and was standing in the doorway and watching me. I did not know what I should do and commenced to tidy the few articles on his dressing-chest, though indeed it showed little enough sign of use. He came up close behind me. I felt his breath come and go quick on my neck. I turned to face him.

'Now that you have made it so nice,' he said, looking away from me towards the bed, 'would you care to lie on it with me?'

This came out in a conversational manner, as if I were on a social call and he was suggesting I might like to take the chair with the softer cushion or might care for a cup of tea.

I should say that this proposal caused me little surprise or alarm. At least, I was not surprised as a proper lady would be – but then, she is not importuned day and night. Such a lady may be surprised, also, to know that her precious gentleman sees in girls of the lower orders, as I belong to, a daily feast, just as a large animal eyes up a smaller one for a possible meal. She does not read it in the books they give her and so cannot know that she is the matter of a French dessert. Such as I am he sees as a dish of mutton-chops. She, he likes to keep for a delicacy, and so, delicate.

'Why, sir, should we lie on it?' I asked.

This may seem coy in me but I knew no other means just then of keeping him from me for a moment while not causing offence. The whole house could be down upon me for offending a lodger. And in any case it is never my wish to displease. I saw quite clear the part that this gentleman, Mr Hazlitt, had fashioned for me, that he should get, for the rate of ten shillings a week, not only his bed but a wench in it. He was not the first of our gentlemen to hope for this additional service, though I was not accustomed to them asking for it so plain. It did cause me some surprise, however, that he assumed a request would serve where another man would employ a wheedling caress, that he was appealing cold to my will as if it were a business we might engage in together. It is true that I may have underestimated how sensible he was and how solitary his spirit. But I did not underestimate his average expectations as a gentleman.

'I should like to sleep with you,' was his answer, as cool as he was before.

This statement afforded me but amusement, for in my position I cannot be ready to take offence. To sleep . . . I imagined what came to me as a comic sight, my head alongside his on the pillow, peacably sleeping like man and wife, his severe face and my smooth one under our nightcaps. But his intention, I knew, was not that we should sleep but that we should be wakened.

He was waiting on my answer. He watched me with a fierce stare. His eyes were dark and hungry in the whiteness of his face. Composed as any girl could be in the situation, I thought it was a face that was grown to be more forbidding and fastidious than it was meant to be or had started out. He was gripping so tight the back of the Waterloo chair that his knuckles were yellow as balls of hard butter. He was a fierce and impetuous character, I saw, and his cool request was not natural to him. At the same time I had a certain disappointment in knowing that a man my father admired to such a degree should think so little of his daughter as to wish to use her as another facility of the house. I intended to make Mr Hazlitt conscious of this by the tone in which I made my reply.

'There is no reason, sir, since I sleep with my sister.'

And, indeed, this was no less than the truth. I have never had the pleasure of the blue room to myself, but have always shared it with one sister or the other. After Martha became Mrs Roscoe, Betsy came in with me. Though I often wish she had not, for she is jumpy in her sleep and fastens her arms tight about me. Still, she serves well enough as a warming-pan in the winter cold.

Perhaps Mr Hazlitt had not made Betsy's acquaintance by this time, for she was not yet accustomed to going into his room to chatter about me and anyone else in the house she had a mind to. Whether he had or no, I was glad to be able to offer her as a pretext. I feared Mr Hazlitt could well be the kind of fellow such as we had a year or so back in Mr Bellew, who lurked in the corners of the stair and once came in search of me in the night.

On receiving my answer, he stepped away without a word into the other room. Anxious to make good my escape, I finished up my dusting with a degree of haste. On my way out through his sitting-room I was obliged to pass him and resolved to do so with my eyes cast down. He was standing with his back to me, looking into the empty grate.

'Sarah,' he called out as I was at the door.

I stopped. 'Yes, sir?'

'I am sorry,' he murmured. 'I hope you will forgive my presumption.'

'I do, sir,' I replied. Well, what else could any girl in that position say?

4

A man who considers himself to be the centre of the world will see but a reflection of his own thoughts and desires in everyone. We are instruments for his use. A woman, especially one who is modest and unassuming as I am – he may say what he likes about me – sees things plain. What I saw was that he was to be pitied.

A woman has a natural inclination to pity and it is sure to bring her more trouble than any passion.

The following morning, at ten o'clock, I went up and was going about my work as before. While I prepared his breakfast-table he sat in the elbow chair with a book in his hands and made a pretence of reading, but I felt his gaze upon me. I made nothing of it. I was in the chamber but a moment, emptying his wash-jug and close-stool into the bucket, when he came again and stood in the doorway, keeping that look upon me. I commenced to mop the floor. He stepped across to his dressing-chest with a clumsy gait and toyed with the articles on it as if seeking to dismiss me. But there was still the bed to be straightened and I was not free to go. In place of dismissing me he looked to me with such a pained smile that I could not but return a shadow of it.

'There is to be nothing, so, between us?' he said.

A man can act at being pitiful with a girl when his

only purpose is to play with her. But I was childish enough yet not to think on this. Conscious of no intent but to console him, I came up and laid a light kiss on his forehead – no more, I am sure, than a girl is used to do for her father or any man she is fond of.

'Your toast will be gone cold, sir,' I remarked in a pleasant tone.

He gave a start, and before I could move off he had gripped my shoulders so I could not move even had I struggled, and he ground his lips into mine in a bruising kiss. Next he was wrapped about me and, though he was quite white in the face so you could think there was not a drop of warm blood in it, his body was burning like a well-fed stove. I was as fearful as a girl could be of being charred, and more than at the edges. Of a sudden then, just when I thought I might suffocate, he loosened his grasp of me and drew back. I saw his expression, which was quite abject, but I saw too that he was glad of his kiss. I made for the door quick as a flash and was on the landing before he could do what he would to stay me.

Betsy was on the stairs cradling and kissing her doll.

'Get up, Betsy, and bring Mr Hazlitt some toast,' I told her.

'You have brought him his toast,' she objected.

'Well, he would like some more,' I replied.

My lip was hot as if it had been brought within an inch of a flaming candle.

'You were a long time in Mr Hazlitt's room,' observed Betsy.

'Well, that is a great deal longer than I shall remain with you if you are going to spy on me like a kitchen-maid and make remarks on my conduct,' I countered.

'I cannot help spying. But I am sorry for making remarks and I will not make them any more,' she said.

'Your mouth would have to be stopped up for you

not to make remarks,' I told her. 'And I should be happy to do it if you will let me.'

'Where are Mr Hazlitt's slops?' asked my mother when I arrived in the kitchen. 'You have forgot to bring the bucket down.'

'Let Lizzie go up for it,' I said, affecting to be tired. 'I am worn out from climbing his stairs.'

'You will forget your own name next,' Mother said. 'Indeed, I declare you are forgetting it already, since you won't consent to be called by it.'

At dinner, she was resolved, in view of what I had said about being worn out, that I would eat some boiled parsnip at least. But Lizzie smothered my plate in the thick brown gravy from the meat-pan and I made only a pretence of eating it.

'Mr Hazlitt is gone out at last,' remarked my mother.

'He is gone to the Fives, I'll bet,' said Cajah.

'What is that?' asked Betsy. I did not care to display any curiosity about Mr Hazlitt's doings.

'It is the games court in Covent Garden. Where the rakes and ratters go.'

'Sarah's face is all flushed up,' observed Betsy, 'to hear Mr Hazlitt is gone with the rakes and ratters.'

'It is flushed because my head aches,' I retorted. 'And in consequence you may wash up the ware.'

I left them to the table and its unsightly freight of dishes and went to my room, where I bolted the door against Betsy and took up my book. But I could not read very well, as I was wondering at Mr Hazlitt and how a learned gentleman could go to such a place as the Fives. I own I was charged with a little excitement to think of him one minute watching me with that fierce look of his and seizing me of a sudden for a kiss – and the next, carrying on as a rake in some scandalous place. And to think of him alone then in his room on his return, bent studious as a churchman over the foolscap and writing essays for the learned journals as if that were his only doing and his only interest. He appeared to me a figure of mystery, and I was curious about him on account of it. I believe now that in such a case a man must always turn out a disappointment.

Soon my mother, who will never consent to leave me alone, sent up Betsy to say I was to go out to the Old Serjeant's, for the Welshman wanted a dish of chops fetched for his dinner. 'She said you are to go, for the air will do you good, and to be always locked up in the house is the best way to sicken,' reported Betsy.

I was glad enough to go on the errand and in the throng of passengers near forgot about Mr Hazlitt. Instead, passing the Inns on Chancery-lane, I hoped to spy Mr Bradley come in or out of its portals and though I did not, my thoughts fell into their habitual reverie of yearning and regret for him who had left me. I do own that this melancholy sensation was waning somewhat by now, however, as I dare say all reasonable loves must as time goes by.

I knew the Welshman cannot abide a wait when he wants his dinner, but still I continued as far as the Strand, seeing as it was so fine, and had an orange for a present from the coster's stall on the corner. I had twopence in my pocket and could easy have paid for it, but the hawker, who was a brown-coloured Latin or some such, would not take my money even if I insisted. 'So fair a young lady should not be obliged to pay for her orange,' he told me. 'She would pay for none of her victuals if I had my way,' he continued, all the while seeking to dazzle me with the whiteness of his teeth against his burnt and fruity complexion. 'If you pass tomorrow,' he said, 'I will see you have another just as juicy.' As was only natural, I took care to avoid the fellow in the future and crossed the street if I saw him, no matter how ardent I might desire an orange, for I had no wish to make a friend of that sort. But I am sure I could be hardly worse off with him than in the company I was thrown into at my own house.

5

As a consequence of what had passed between me and Mr Hazlitt, there was none of the common sport with us, the meaning looks and little falsities of hidden sentiment that serve well to keep a pair apart. It was all out in the open from the first, what he wanted from me. And with his backing off, that he was ready to forgo it. It gave me the illusion of a knowledge of him that seemed to make our dealings plain, and worse, caused me to see him in the light of a friend. There is a frankness in such a case between you and the gentleman. It is as if a large obstacle such as a closet has been removed from the centre of the room and in place of weaving one's way around it one can move free about and do one's work. What is inevitable to be offered by a gentleman to a girl of inferior place in life has been offered. And though it seldom brings an end to the gentleman's advances, the girl's refusal of them – should she wish to refuse – has been made and this makes putting up with them easier.

On the morning following the kiss, Mr Hazlitt greeted me in a quiet and friendly manner. He remained seated in his easy-chair as I laid out his breakfast-things and placed the kettle on the spirit-lamp to boil up afresh as my mother had instructed. 'He will not have his tea brought up but must have it made new above,' she said. 'And ensure that his jug is always filled up with water as he must have his Bohea to drink all the while as he writes.' It was she who had been seeing to him while I was at the Roscoes' – though I dare say she remained free of such invitations from him as I received.

I could feel Mr Hazlitt's eyes steadfast upon me but did not dare to look upon him direct for shyness at meeting them. However, with a few stolen glances I saw he had made his toilet, his hair was brushed back from his high forehead, as neat as it could be made, and his sallow complexion had a rosy tint from its plunge in the basin.

'Do you like to read, Sarah?' he demanded of a sudden.

'I do, sir, when I have time enough,' I said in reply.

I would have liked to tell him I was resolved to increase the capacity of my mind and force my sentiments to wither to a manageable size. I was still childish enough to fancy this was what reading and learning did for a person. But my tongue would not unstick itself to utter anything more than it had.

Withdrawing to his chamber, I dressed his tumbled bed and neatened his clothes and the few things he had left scattered about. I gave some little time to polishing. When I returned to his room I found he had wet his tea. He was standing by the table, as if ready to sit in to his breakfast. I moved towards the door. He stayed me with a hand on my arm. It was a light touch, not presuming.

'I should like to give you something, Sarah, should you be kind enough to accept it.'

'What is it, sir?'

'A little book of mine.'

'A book you have written yourself, sir?'

He smiled. It was an indulgent smile that lent his

expression a sweetness which I had not seen on his face before. I was surprised to be driven to suspect by it that he might have a certain regard for me.

'It is my most recent volume, and a slight thing. But I hope to improve on it in the future. And no doubt you may find it tedious, as the subject can be of little interest to a girl. But I should like you to have it. I take the presumption of believing it a book that, as a daughter of this house, you might not be unhappy to have in your keeping.'

'I am sure I shall be glad to take it,' I told him. And I was indeed, for I regarded his words as a compliment to my father – though I was apprehensive that my understanding might not be good enough to take in such a work.

In the hand that was hanging out of sight behind his back, he had the volume ready to present to me, waiting on my acceptance. Now he brought it forward. The volume was slender, I was relieved to see, and bound very handsome in red. I took it and read aloud the title. '*Political Essays. William Hazlitt.*' I feared I might not be able to make a great deal of it but I was happy to admire it.

'It is a small token,' he said, soft-toned, 'of my shame and my regret at having offended you yesterday.'

'It was no more than a common offence, sir,' I protested. Though whether I had been offended or not I was unable to rightly say just then.

'You are too gentle and modest to take offence,' he murmured. 'And I misjudged you.'

I thanked him for the book and was once more about to leave him, when he again stayed me.

'You are not going, Sarah, without granting me a kiss?'

The question was not assuming. I might easy have refused. Indeed, I am sure he expected a refusal. He made his request in quite a light tone. But his expression was hapless, as if a kiss was the thing he wanted most dear in all the world. I thought his presumption in asking for it made some mockery of what he had claimed to be sorry about. But all the same I reached up to him for his cheek, not knowing how, faced with that look and holding his book under my arm, I could refuse. I thought it a simple thing to give if it would make him happy.

I met his lips, for he was not content with a little peck on his cheek. This morning they were soft and dry and diffident. I felt him tremble. It was not an amorous kiss, nor pressing, nor the common kiss of intent. I had the impression it meant something above the ordinary to him.

I stepped aside. 'I will be glad, Mr Hazlitt, I am sure, to read anything you write and should choose to show me,' I said. Then I left him.

6

Mr Hazlitt was not a particular impressing man, at least of the kind to appeal to a girl – and now it is certain he is not. But he was a singular man and this made me feel warm towards him. His pale complexion could colour in an instant from the heat of the fire or my nearness or the impulses of his temperament, so its alterations would always present a spectacle. And though a girl ought not comment on such a thing, or so Martha says, he had a good well-turned leg. That came, I suppose, from all the walking he did, whether in the town or the country. His eyes were of a generous size and could glow soft or fierce as the mood took him. I fancy his was a poet's eye more than a scholar's, and I am sure that if he were to put down his swooning and flaming moods in rhyming verse like Lord Byron he might be better liked and his friends not made so wretched.

I can vouch that he certainly carried on like a poet in his pride and arrogance which was expressed in his case by his absence of vanity and dignity. The manner of his dress was not in the least respectable. You could think he went for the purchase of his garments to the oldclothesmen in Holywell Street, so shabby and unfashionable were they. Neglecting to send out his linen to be washed, he thought nothing of stepping abroad in a neckcloth three days old and with his boots dirty. I am not acquainted with Mr Wordsworth or any of his poetic friends but I am sure that if he is a poet itself he is a tidy and sober man, or else he could not be respected as he is. Oh, Mr Hazlitt made every pretence of being sober. He did not drink gin or ale and took care to tell me so as he was proud of his abstaining. But of course it turned out, as Mr Roscoe told us, that he had drunk his life's share all at once in his younger years and had to keep off it now or be destroyed. He did not yet display the consequences of his long accretion of years when he came to live with us. His brows were then well shaped and handsome – now they are become as wild as a Hampstead hedge. I suppose men of genius may keep the complexion and shine of youth because their blood courses through them from all that explosive activity of the brain. Although my mother said that if you were to bleed Mr Hazlitt, tea might gush out in place of blood and he was on the way to turning yellow like a Chinaman.

This is a charge Mr Hazlitt lays to my mother – that she gossiped about him in the kitchen, just as he says she gossiped about all the lodgers. Let him suggest to us what other topic we might pick, when we are in such close contact with our lodgers' persons and their tastes, and toil all day to keep them comfortable. Do we have time, let him ask himself, for any other acquaintance to interest ourselves in, but they? The whole day, it is true, though I do not see why we must make any apology for it, there was little else we spoke of.

'Has Mr Griffith had his tray?' 'Mr Follett wants his linen changed.' 'Mr Tilditch expects his tea at four.'

I am sure, however, that Mother never spoke of him with disrespect to Mr Patmore or any of his friends who called at the house. This cannot be said of him – who has not only talked of us but put us in a book for people to read who do not even know us and are unlikely to trouble themselves to make up their own minds on our conduct. By this treachery he has made us, who remained his friends despite all, his enemies. We might have managed him better perhaps. But we enjoyed no great experience in the ways of keeping a lodging-house. We were not born to the business. My father had taken 9 Southampton Buildings but a few years before we were landed with Mr Hazlitt. It was still a novelty with us, more a daily excitement than a trade. I declare we had the notion that we were a class all to ourselves.

As for me, it is false to claim I will consent to kiss any man who asks, no matter what William Hazlitt says. He says it only because he had a kiss from me of a morning. But what was I to do, as he would not sit to his breakfast until he had his kiss. Seeing his tea was in danger of growing dank as the Serpentine from the long infusion, I might consent to kiss him. He had the bearing, if not the dress, of a gentleman. My father admired him. Though I own I did not kiss him for my father's sake.

I think I had a right to kiss any man I had a mind to. Was this not the one power in my possession, to kiss or not to kiss, as I wished, whosoever should request it? Let the fine ladies give up this power if they want. They may have something to gain by the refusal.

My sister begged me to remember that indeed I was not a servant but an assistant to my mother in her own house and business. And that I had every hope of improving my position, as she herself had done, and the prospect of the commanding of servants of my own. I considered this very hopeful in her. I was not wise and virtuous as she was and I was more given over to sentiment. She was also fortunate. In the case of Mr Bradley, Lady Luck had not smiled on me and I could see nothing in my future except the mill-horse round of carrying up and down the dark lengths of stairs all day.

Tea-trays and bug-trays, slop-pails, ash-pails and night-buckets. Brooms, jugs, coal-scuttles, kettles and kindling. Ale-mugs and dinner dishes when our lodgers were not disposed to dine at the chop-house.

I am to be faulted, it looks, for stopping an hour or two from carrying this or that hither and thither and electing to sit an instant with Mr Hazlitt or anyone else I choose. Should I not enjoy the rooms I make up and keep warm and neat? Have I not as much need as anyone of a snatch of civil company? I had hours enough to endure in the clattery vaporous kitchen with Lizzie gabbling some nonsense at me and Baby to be watched and Mother urging me to some chore or other.

7

First he must have his morning kiss. I believe he stood before the glass, readying his appearance to meet me, for his hair would be combed, though it was awry at any other time. As to his insistence that I could not leave him to breakfast alone but must keep him company, well, he would have starved of hunger if I did not agree. Once he had drained the teapot I would fill it up again and he would settle back to another, conversing all the while. Mr Hazlitt could spout an infinity when he chose.

As I made up his fire and his bed and folded his clothes, for he threw them down anywhere as he pleased, he would sit in the easy-chair by the sparking fire and talk or read to me, though just as often he came to a stop to watch me too. I declare I soon knew as much about the game of fives, and rackets too, as Cajah did, who could go about and watch the play as he chose at the courts in Saint Martin's Street, for Mr Hazlitt was never done talking about the games to me. I learned all about Mr Cavanagh, the greatest player of fives there ever was, according to Mr Hazlitt, who, from the way he praised him, mourned his passing more than he did that of his own father, who was but new-dead when he came to us, just as young Mr Cavanagh was too.

'The ball flew from his hand, Sarah, with the same force as from a racket,' he would exclaim. Why, when he went to write about the Indian Jugglers, he soon fell to writing about Cavanagh instead, which I think must be a flaw in the essay, for surely you should stick fast to your subject once you have embarked on it and be as forceful about it as Mr Cavanagh was with his ball.

Mr Hazlitt was quite conscious of his habit of digressing. 'Here I fear I digress, Sarah,' he would announce as he read me something of what he had written. He fell into a digression so often I was driven to think he regarded his fault with approval as much as regret, otherwise he would have mended it. In the case of Mr Cavanagh, I am sure that the fact of them both being Irishmen had a deal to do with Mr Hazlitt's enthusiasm for him.

Yet, despite his faults as an essayist, having Mr Hazlitt talk at me was like having a tutor of my own in the house, I fancied then, such as young ladies have. He did not teach me French or drawing, it is true, or any ladies' accomplishments. But neither did he by any means talk only of fives and rackets. He might begin on that topic but very quick he would divert to another subject, for instance that of Mr Keats, who played at fives too and who he believed to be a tender and delicate versifier – though not a great one, as he wanted strength and vigour. I am sure he was correct on that score, as at this time Mr Keats was a poor sick fellow gone off to Italy for the good of his health and has since passed away.

He lectured me in serious subjects like the history of the French – though it seemed to me a sad one, since we trounced them well and proper and they are but a rebelly race. I was also instructed on painters and poets and the beauties of their work, which is surely more useful than any of your French or drawing in black and white in the Japanese style. At that time I could have told you anything you wished to know about Mr Reynolds or Mr Correggio or Mr Rembrandt. I knew they were men of genius and that to only look at a scene they painted was to fancy yourself in it.

Well, having the opportunity to learn from one who my father declared was 'among the finest of London's literary men', I was glad of it. And was not proud enough to fancy that such a brilliant man as he should consent to be generous as he was without wishing to take some pleasures of his own. I regarded it in the light of a trade, or the bargain you make when you buy French eggs in the market. They may be small but at threepence a dozen they are a fair price for the size. The result was that I was often not out of my mob-cap and morning-gown till it was near dinner-time.

However scandalous he now pretends to regard my behaviour, I don't believe I acted in any way different from how any young lady would in my position. I do not believe that a tutor and his young lady, as they sit together day after day in an elegant schoolroom, don't kiss and fondle. The proximity is not conducive to avoiding it, even should she wish it. And even if she is inclined to be plain as I am – though men have often spoken to the contrary – why, Mr Hazlitt was continual speaking of my looks, to the point of putting me in tears – any man, be he young or old, is keen to court any young lady proximate.

Stroking my hair all the while, he would tell me about his friends and his enemies, how this one was a good fellow, and that one a blackguard. They were for the most part editors in the magazines, or writing for them. He was passing fond of Mr Lamb, the literary man, to whose house at Mitre Court he often went to dine. He used to declare that you could always depend on Lamb. It was Mr Lamb who kept him supplied with his quantities of steel nibs, as there was a great store of them at the India Office, where Mr Lamb had a nice position.

In general he sat and tried to coax me to stand by him. But in the heat of his discourse he might jump to his feet of a sudden to walk about or to demonstrate to me his handling of the racket at the Fives. Seizing the ash-pan, he would swing it to right and left, swiping at an imaginary ball, and leaping into the air. More than once he knocked a lighted candle from its socket. He might well have set the house ablaze. But I was lively and got to it and it only sputtered and went out.

But he was not often inclined to be boisterous. He would be quite tame as he read from his latest work he was engaged with, such as a critique for the magazine of a play he had seen. Then he would beg me to come and sit by him and to know my opinion. My opinion was in general admiring as he wrote vivid and with an impressive fervour, though I own I sometimes found it hard to follow what he wrote. Is it not very unjust now that he should use his genius to such effect as to insult me, whom he used to call his queen? But he has as much fondness for a queen as he has for a Tory so I might have known from the start his endearments were tainted with hypocrisy.

He made a great show of valuing my opinions. When I did venture to murmur a criticism in place of praise, this gave rise to the first of our arguments. It concerned the poet Wordsworth. Maybe he was not fair to Mr Wordsworth, I objected, when he wrote that he was egoistic and knew nothing of the world. 'I always thought,' I said, 'that a poet's imagination supplies him with as much as he needs to know.' I believe, though I did not say it, that he would have liked to strip from Mr Wordsworth the name of genius which he enjoys in all quarters.

At this he stood up from his place and paced about

the room. Then, stiff as a poker, he informed me that I could know nothing about the matter. 'I trust you will not object, Sarah, when I say that you are but a female, made for the domestic sphere. Your intellect was neither formed nor developed, by nature nor by education, to judge such matters.'

I do not say this was unfair in him. But I was alarmed by his tone, when after all he had elicited my opinion, and made to leave the room. At this, he rushed to the door to forestall me. With the threat of tears damping his eyes he entreated me not to be angry. My greatest charm, he assured me, was my submissive nature and my serenity and the impression I gave that I could not be moved by anything but by sentiment or the sweet converse which we enjoyed.

'I will be made happy, my dear Sarah, and so too will you, if you leave the labour of philosophy to such poor creatures as we men are. You can have no wish to displease me and give up your feminine talents of loyalty and admiration by taking on the qualities of a bluestocking. You do wish to please me, don't you, Sarah?'

'I do, sir,' I agreed, to calm him and to get away from his suffering look. And indeed it was the truth, as to please the gentlemen of the house was always my purpose, in so far as it did not go against me in my health or my reputation.

8

It is a blessed thing, I used to fancy, to be able to bend your head over a foolscap and cover it in words we fumble for in our speech, and then send it out into the world so that thousands of people may wonder at it. I used to think Mr Hazlitt blessed in the way of all men of letters. My father holds it to be blessed, and my mother in consequence affected to, though in truth she hardly believes anyone or anything holy. I have such a mother as goes carelessly into the street wearing her mob-cap and her apron and wonders why I run after her with her bonnet. 'If 'tis not the fashion, I can make it the fashion,' she grumbles as I tie the ribbons under her chin with a nice bow.

It may be objected that I put myself in the way of his advances by not getting out of doing for Mr Hazlitt. If I had I might have saved myself from his harassments. It might be objected that my mother, had I told her of them, would have served him herself and forbidden me to enter his rooms and instructed me to turn back down the stairs the minute there was a danger of finding myself alone with him. But I have a mother who thinks this kind of conduct only manly in her lodgers and laughs at it and expects me to laugh at it too and presumes that every girl has grown up with a shell like a beetle's that keeps her safe from attempts at seduction and commonplace entreaties.

I do not think she can have known feelings as intense as Mr Hazlitt's, nor how fragile a thing a girl's carapace can be when she is faced with them.

As for my father, he is a quiet, hard-working man whose first pleasure is a long perusal of his newspaper, and after that his domestic peace and the modest upkeep of his family. No, Mother would see no reason at all to deprive Mr Hazlitt, after Father's persuasion of her that he was such an imposing personage, of my company should he be so kind as to desire it. She would only laugh at my fears – though indeed they did not appear half so grave that I ever thought of speaking of them until it was too late – and she would declare they were fears the daughter of a lodging-house had no entitlement to. Caution and prudence are my only entitlements.

'You are a good girl, Sal, and will be so, I hope, until you are married. Then you may be as bold as you like.' This was the only advice my mother saw fit to give. And it was only for the sake of custom that she gave it at all. She has no proper opinions on the matter of a girl's reputation as it is expected to stand in the 1820s, when we are meant to be twice as moral as she was used to, nor of how her conduct might compromise us. She hardly accepts that manners are different now than when she was young, and that a girl must be wiser than she once was in the lax days of the old king. Also she married up to a more respectable situation than she was born into and carried her lower ways with her.

My mother's only anxiety concerning me was my health, on account of my lack of appetite. In consequence, when she thought of it, she encouraged me to take a turn in the streets for a bout of exercise and a breath of fresh air. If you may call it fresh air, what we have in London, for they say it is grievous tainted in comparison to what they get in the country. It does make you wonder, if so, why all the country folk crowd in from there to get a taste of ours. Yet, if we had it sweet itself, it would do no good, for when it is summer the horses, who must be near as numerous as the people, set up clouds of dust from their hoofs to stifle the breath. And in other seasons, there is the damp fog to saturate it, and mire instead of a path to tread in.

But often I did not care what was the air I breathed, even if I were muddied and jostled, as long as it was not the air in the house, and did not mind how long I tramped. Sometimes I could go as far as Saint James's. Once I footed it to the Green Park to look at the cows. When a girl goes that far, surely she is entitled to sit down on a bench for a rest? Well, if I made so bold as to sit, I was likely to be pestered, by one fellow or another who presumed my sole purpose in being there was for him to make up to.

There is a great deal for a girl to put up with, so many snares and traps lying in wait for her in the shape of men. That is why she is obliged to go about with her eyes cast down and her shawl wrapped tight around her, playing the part of a dim and dutiful creature whose mind is on nothing but the tasks awaiting her at home. I dare say to walk in the country must be an improvement in that respect too, for it is emptier. Mr Hazlitt loved to walk in the country. But he never went to wander in the park in my company. He kept me for his indoor amusement.

It is plain to see, he is hardly a gentleman, or he would not have kept me hidden away. And yet I dare say neither he nor my mother are to be blamed, for I own I was quite content then in the mornings to be seeing Mr Hazlitt and would not have been pleased to yield him up.

Remarking how his ink made jagged stains on the writing-table, I thought I must bring him a thick cloth to spread as a bed for his inkpot, so his pen might drip as it liked. I cut a piece for the purpose from the old blue velvet that used to hang at the parlour window. I brought him too the tea-caddy with a dog for its knob to keep his supply of Bohea. When he remarked such little touches of comfort, he made no objection. Indeed, he told me he was grateful to know I thought of him sometimes when I was not in his room.

9

'Were you used to breakfast alone, sir, before you came to us?' I ventured to ask, now he had been with us several weeks. But timid, since you can never tell whether a gentleman will object to an enquiry. I considered him indeed the kind of man liable to resent a girl being inquisitive, so it was a mark of my confidence in him that I asked it. It is not general in me to ask personal questions of the lodgers.

'I have not always been alone,' he said with a frown. His curls were damp about his forehead as he had just come from dipping his face in the basin. Taking my hand in a coaxing way, he caressed it as if he found it beautiful. I rub wax in my hands to smooth them, but they are not, I think, smooth nor beautiful.

'I once had a wife, Sarah,' he continued after a little.

'Is she long dead, sir?'

He gave a chuckle. 'Oh, she is not dead but hale as a body could wish.'

'Did she offend you, sir?'

'I fear the fault was as often on my side. We like one another well enough. But we will not do as man and wife, so we live apart.' Here he looked at me in an entreating manner. 'But when we lived together I declare I never took such pleasure in my tea and toast with her as I do with you. And I don't believe I was ever as pained when she was not inclined.'

It did not surprise me that he had a wife, nor that he could take her or leave her at his breakfast-table. He was of an age when men are not only husbands of so long a standing that the joys of the position are staled, but are often widowers too. And a man who is used to being a bachelor would hardly be so forward and frank as he. He recited for me a part of an essay, which he had just composed, and proposed to title *On Effeminacy of Character*. And with eyes agleam and stopped breath wanted to know then whether I thought it good. My inward opinion was that I feared he was over-harsh with such characters, for they seemed harmless in their hesitations and timidities if you compared them with some others more robust. I wondered who it was he was describing, for it seemed a portrait of some writing-acquaintance that he did not name, and for good reason. I also thought effeminacy a luxury and a vice that such a girl as I could be in no danger of acquiring. No one in our house would be at liberty to hesitate or shilly-shally for much above an hour before a lodger came clamouring at the kitchen door to demand a service.

I assured him there were excellent notions in it. However, I did venture to wonder whether his title of *Table Talk* for the volume in which all the essays were to be assembled might suggest a work of slight importance. I own I objected to the title thinking to impress him, though it was too no more than the truth as our table talk below stairs is in general of a trivial nature.

Up he leapt at this like I were a bee that had stung him, and clasped his head in his hands and paced about, crashing now into the stool, then the fire-irons. You would think I had dealt him a mortal wound. And you can be sure I saw again my mistake, that I should not venture to be a critic, certainly at least without at first paying an effusion of compliments.

'But you must approve it,' he exclaimed. 'Why, it is for you I write, Sarah. It is all for you. I never had anyone to write for before. Yes, yes, it is the truth. I believe I would never write a word again were it not for you.'

I own I was passing pleased to hear Mr Hazlitt say such a thing. Grasping my hand in his, he told me that he might have written for his wife, but she had gone against him in everything.

'I beg you, do not play the kind of wife with me, Sarah, who would tell her husband how to write, so he is led to thinking he wields his pen only at her bidding. I had a wife who judged my work with the detachment of some tavern acquaintance. I could not bear it were you to attempt to ape that style. She is intellectually proud, but her understanding is limited, though she does not know it. Now we live apart because she was never wife to me as I dreamed a wife might be . . .'

Here he lowered his voice and his gaze. I removed my hand and went to clear away the tray. Following close, he hung by my side. His indignation at my presumption in doubting his title was past and now he assumed a pleading manner.

'You do not hold it against me, do you, Sarah?'

'What could I hold against you, sir?'

'That I have a wife.'

'It is nothing to me whether you have a wife or not,' I told him straight.

What could it mean to me? That I was conscious of a blankness of feeling, which lasted but a moment, or the brief bleakness of spirit indicative of a small disappointment, does not by any means infer that I was grievous disappointed to hear Mr Hazlitt was a married gentleman.

Feelings are independent, often unreasonable things that can exist, like wives, apart from oneself. They may live but they need not be significant. How many feelings are there and how many their different degrees that you can be subject to throughout a day, or even in an hour? Rage, when slop-water splashes on to the boards from the close-stool because you have stumbled over your skirts. Dismay, when Lizzie plucks a piece of fat meat from the pot and chews it standing up, hearty and noisy, with her broken teeth. The thin pleasure at tying up your hair and putting on your bonnet to go out, and finding a vacant bench in the garden at Lincoln's Inn, shaded by foliage, to sit on. Thinking of your love, and fancying you are loved yet, before the knowledge descends again that you are not. The melancholy feeling when night is falling and Mother is sparing the candles. The weakness at Cajah's grabbing hold of you, though that is hardly a feeling, rather the lack of it. The little delight when Baby would consent to take his spoon.

All feelings such as these are to be held in check, hourly, daily. That is a girl's first duty. If, that is, she means to be regarded as a lady, an object of respect, and a reproach to those who call out to her uncouth on the stairs or try to take her arm and lead her off in the street with a promise of ninepence.

IO

On the next morning, Mr Hazlitt was waiting for me all impatient just inside the door, as if his very life depended on getting his tea and toast. But in place of sitting up to his table when I set the tray down, he was restless, pacing up and down and talking, though I could hardly attend to what he said as the weather was turned cold and I had the fires to light again. The chimney being so long disused, his would not draw, and I was already late as the Welshman had been longer abed than was his habit.

'I fear I offended you yesterday, Sarah. But if I appeared angry I did not mean it. A writer can be too fond of his work at times, as a loving father can be overindulgent with his child and lets him run about . . . But you must never be afraid to tell me what you are thinking. I like nothing better than to know your thoughts on any subject' – here he gave his pained smile – 'and particularly what you may be pleased to think of me. I am not accustomed to the company of young ladies; I am rendered brutal by the company of men who like to think low of me . . . I have a wife, but she is wife no longer in my heart, wife though she be in law. Yes, and a son too. I should like him to meet you,

Sarah, before very long . . .' He stopped and looked long at me.

'Will you consent to meet him? He is a little dear chap – and was all in the world I cared for, until I met you. And I declare he should know you, he should like to know you, as I do. He is called William, like his father and his grandfather too. Ah, that was another too I cared for, my dear father, who but lately went to his rest . . . Have I spoken to you of him, Sarah? He was my first and best teacher, and my friend in all matters of justice and good.'

I assured him that he had indeed spoken of the old man and, in a mumble, for I do not care to speak of such matters, that I was sorry he had lost him when he had loved him so. I think he did not care to hear it either just then, for he resumed his pacing forward and back.

'Yesterday, after you left me, I found myself in Covent Garden oppressed and distracted by the conviction that I had offended you and had lost, as much as I had your kisses, your good opinion of me. I went to the Fives but had no taste for the game. I could hardly swing my racket, it was a leaden weight attached to my arm. All on account of you, Sarah. And in the evening I dined at Lamb's and he wondered that I was downcast and would not converse, so that he became downcast too, though he had been entertaining before. So I told him and Mary, who is his sister, all about you, Sarah, how good you are, and sweet, and that I am not worthy of you. And they assured me they believed it, for they are excellent people and possess none of the natural prejudices.'

Mr Lamb must indeed be the kindest of men, but among the most foolish too, for he keeps his sister, who went mad and killed their mother, loose in his house. Sometimes she goes mad again and then she is confined while he waits patient for her to be well. Mr Roscoe speaks very high of his kindness and good humour despite all. But I did not consider Mr Hazlitt to be so kind, speaking in one breath of his horror at offending me and the next all lofty of those who would be entitled to have natural prejudices against me.

I cannot say I never heard such love-talk as his before. Such is the talk of many a man when he is taken in the ordinary way with a girl. Especially the kind of girl whose affections he does not consider it immodest or indiscreet to discuss. Once, I own, when I heard something of the like from Mr Bradley, I was all too ready to believe in such talk. However, ready as I was to disbelieve Mr Hazlitt, his extravagance had a fervour in it that impressed and indeed could alarm me a little sometimes.

'You are an angel, Sarah, sent to me from Heaven,' he declared. 'For now I believe in the possibility of Heaven. And though it may be found only here on earth, that is all to the better. It grieves me that my dealings with you have not been as they should be. When an angel floats into a man's chamber unannounced, in the guise of his serving-maid, he should fall down upon his knees . . .'

Coming to his senses, he looked at the smouldering fire and the teapot gurgling on the lamp. 'Come, Sally, sit. I shall take my tea.'

It was a poor cup by this time, from the dingy look of it, but he drank it off like a man wandering in a barren China desert.

In general I preferred to stand. It was not my place to sit like a visitor in a gentleman's chamber. He would not touch the buttered toast I had brought up but caught and held fast my fingers as he drank.

'Forgive me, Sally, if I offend you,' he said at last and loosened his hold. 'But I have never met as sweet a girl as you. I would never harm such a girl. You know that, don't you?'

I was childish enough then to think the only harm he could do me was to address me as Sally as if I were a kitchen-maid.

He pulled me close to him, not rough as another man might, and which I would have been well prepared for, but cool like he had come to a decision to do it. He spoke low but firm. 'Won't you sit on my knee, Sarah?'

It would be deceitful of me to pretend that I did as he asked with any great reluctance, although to say that it was something I desired would be also untrue. I had no firm opinions as to my wishes – and whether any girl could have in the circumstances, I doubt. When we have so little independence in life, we can hardly have independence in thought. His wishes, you see, were both firm and strong, and it is a girl's way, whatever she may pretend to believe, to do as she is asked to by a gentleman. And it must not be left out of the reckoning that it was no little comfort to me, in the rather forlorn state in which I then was – nothing though it was to my present one – to feel the heat of a man so close and his quickening heart and his arm tight around my waist. To find my society so much courted was grateful to me. I would certainly have stayed him if he had tried anything untoward. But he did not, nor attempt to play with my bodice – though later he did – but confined his attentions to a soft and watery gaze that played upon my countenance as all the while he stroked my hair under my mob-cap and assured me I was such a pretty one.

II

I suppose I must be pretty, as Mr Hazlitt was by no means the first to tell me so. But to a man, any girl his eye falls upon is to be considered pretty, to be played with, and cajoled, if she is not careful, into catastrophe. A man may be a girl's plaything too. But it is a game at which she must be as disciplined as Mr Hazlitt is about his writing, and as serious, for it can be a game to the death for a girl and she must keep herself in check.

I may be low-sized – but that need be no bad thing when a girl is slender as I am. My complexion wants colour but it is clear and my hair is fair, which gentlemen I think prefer to dark, though it is rather lank and needs curling with papers. I am told I am uncommon graceful in my movements and I have attempted to perfect this for want of any other distinction.

My eyes are remarkable – but, I fear, only to their detriment. They are of a monotonous green hue and the blacks blink and ache in the light, and are but pinpoints in consequence, so they lack the meaning and expression that is wished for in a young lady but to my mind is found at its best in timid dogs. Betsy says they are glassy but a pretty colour for glass and she wishes she could pluck them out like stones. My mouth, I believe, is good, and my profile too, should anyone wish to immortalise me in paint. I might do quite well for a silhouette.

I have not the self-love to give a flattering description, nor the genius to rhapsodise myself in words, nor the learning to encapsulate them in a fine quotation. Mr Hazlitt has such skills but he was not inclined to use them in my case. His eulogy is the cold destructive one of disillusion. In his youth Mr Hazlitt was a painter but gave it up for want of the painting genius. He found he had the genius for words instead.

Oh, that he had continued in the painting way. He might have immortalised me in the harmless garb of paint for all I care. He could have done me glassy eyes and all. Why, he could have made me ugly as he liked, as it would have been for a few eyes only. And after the likeness had hung a while in some house I never frequent, such as Mr Lamb's or Mr Montague's, it would soon be sent up, for want of beauty, to the cook's garret. There it could hang as a lesson to her of the depths to which a want of prudence and modesty might bring her should she not devote herself to her pans. I should not care, for it would have no other existence. Unlike a book, which is copied by the thousand for a thousand eyes to ogle. While the cook might soon turn the picture's face to the wall or keep it in the dust under her bed, and it would be seen no more.

As it is, Mr Patmore and Mr Lamb and Mr Lamb's mad sister – who suffers less ignominy than I do though as a murderer she must deserve it more – and Mr Montague and both the Mr Roscoes, and a thousand others, and thousands more next year and the year after that, may keep my gruesome image on their shelves and gloat upon it as an image of depravity, and look on it anew any hour of the day or night they please.

12

'Why do you hang about Mr Hazlitt? You are always in his room.'

My mother was given now to making this complaint, not chiding nor fearful of my virtue, such as perhaps a better mother might. She complained because she was chafing at my absence from the kitchen and considered I was not often enough at her disposal to run errands for her. To fetch the jug of beer from the eating-house for her dinner, to oblige Baby to take his gruel, to clear the breakfast-trays and sweep the stairs. This last task, however, I began to be now let off and was entitled to leave it to Betsy or Lizzie, seeing as I am not a common servant, which is what I informed my mother, and so do not like to be seen by the gentlemen in the disguise of one.

'I like his conversation,' I protested.

'Well, Sal, I dare say it may do you good to learn something from him,' she said. 'But take care you do not learn too much.'

What she meant by that was I should not learn enough to be disgraced. But I had learned enough for that already from her darling Cajah, though she did not know it. Why, since we were little more than children, well before he had taken to going about the town playing the rake, my brother Cajah was always lying in wait for me in hidden corners, seeking to explore me. He had let me alone for a time, as I expect he had other fish to fry, but now there he was by the wall where it is dark and secret under the mulberry when I was coming back from a visit to the small house.

'Come here to me, Sal,' he hissed. He pulled me close. Winter had come on for good and all and it was an evening cold and drear. Dead leaves were falling every moment on us and settling on his hair and shoulders before a gust took them and they tumbled on to the wet ground.

'What do you do with the old gentleman?' he demanded. 'Do you do with him what you were used to do with me? You are always in his room.'

'I do nothing with him,' I answered. 'I am only fond of his conversation.'

'I believe he is mighty fond of you, Sal, and not of your conversation. Take care you do not talk to him of me. He would think a deal less of you then.'

'I don't know what you are talking of.' I did know, very well.

'Ah, Sal. You are getting the hang of it. How to deceive a fellow.' He laughed. 'That will stand to you, no doubt. I've learned you well.'

I made to get away. I had no wish to remain with Cajah when he gripped me so urgent under the cold and gaudy sky.

He held my shoulder and stayed me fast and fumbled with my bodice. 'Let me see if your bubbies have grown,' he whispered. 'You may please me if you please old Hazlitt.'

I allowed him a feel but only for an instant. I had no choice, he was holding me fast. But when his grip slackened, I cut loose and ran to the kitchen and there I was safe. Betsy was measuring out for a plum cake, my mother by her side, instructing her. She bade me ready the trays for the morning and I was glad enough to do it.

I am no longer frightened by my brother and would not now stand for him for an instant. There was a time I had to, when Martha was entertaining Mr Roscoe in the parlour and he would slip into our bed and oblige me to let him explore me under my clothes and to hold his weapon, as he called it, and assure him he was well-armed while he groaned in a transport. That time is well past.

I should not be surprised if all brothers, even those of a better class than mine, use their sisters in such a way. Cajah held it to be well known among brothers that they have a right to make free with their sisters, for their mutual education, just as long as they do not intend to ruin them for the husbands they will have later on. Since a brother and his sister are so close, he said, it is only natural. And he held that any husband should be glad of a wife who came to him not burdened by ignorance nor alarmed by what he wanted of her.

But I think it would be unnatural in any girl who loves her husband to be alarmed, no matter how little she knows. I was hardly alarmed even by Cajah. I was only alarmed by him being my brother and his want of entitlement, in spite of his claims, to play with me as he did. And seeing him about the house and being conscious of what we did in secret. It went on for longer than it ought because I did not know how to put a stop to it and felt helpless and obedient as a spinning-top in his hands. A man may make a toy of a woman and she may be ashamed and even hate him – and herself more than him – but she is under his spell and cannot break free. That is a thing I learned from Cajah.

But the worst that came out of it was that in consequence I was lax with the gentlemen. It was on account of Cajah, I fear, that Mr Bradley left our house and gave me up, as I did not play the innocent with him but allowed him the same freedoms I allowed my brother. The consequence was that he came to consider me a light character. To fall out of my station, that is all too easy for me because it is not an established nor a precise one. I might, if my actions are appropriate, be regarded as a lady, if a humble one, or so Martha insists. Or I might drop away into the depths and be a miserable wretch walking the lanes of Whitechapel, or, at best, a painted one parading the Colonnades.

That was a more important thing I learned, though I learned it too late. A girl must hold back and run blushing from a man, much as she loves him, as though she were only that week born. She must deceive him as to her wishes and intentions, and especially as to her former experiences. Then he can see her, which he is pleased to, in a heavenly light. As an angel, hardly human at all − choosing to disregard her capacity to black his boots and boil his beef − he will love her to distraction. Otherwise, he is like to put her out in the morning, which he is also pleased to, along with his slop-basin.

Oh yes, he may take great pleasure in his spontaneities, his temptings, his declarations that she must be his or he will die. And in response she must be as impenetrable and ungiving as the Tower of London, as if the stays in her whalebone bind tight her heart and her brain as well. But lacking that wisdom, I could hardly have the will to stick to it.

13

Not knowing what is my place in the world – this must be the principal cause, I am sure, of my misfortunes. I may be put in the way of gentlemen as much as any lady could hope, but only because I carry pails forward to them and back, and their trays, and black their boots when Lizzie is not to be found or is humped over her smoky pots and steamy tubs in the kitchen. I might be called a beast of burden or a Jill-of-all-trades, but never a lady. And even were I to sit all day long in the parlour in my silk gown working adages or flowers or calls to virtue with my needle, I do not think I would be regarded as such. I did indeed sit in the parlour when I felt like it and plied my needle, but only upon a pile of worn linen that Mother wanted mending.

I am not a personage Miss Austen would ever think of putting in a book. A girl like me would be of no interest to her. She would never stoop to write of the smoke and all the thousands of women who shuffle in it through the streets wrapped up in their poor shawls and their wretchedness. For all that each one of them is as important to herself as are any of her spoiled young ladies, who have nothing to worry them only whether the landowner or the lieutenant has the better looks or money to recommend him for a husband.

My sister is, I dare say, a lady because she is now Mrs Roscoe. She may be pleased on occasion to engage in unladylike kitchen doings such as the making of Mr Roscoe's favourite puddings, but this is only an amusement to her. She has servants to do it if she is not inclined. And she can scold them as she pleases. Here, it is Lizzie who feels free to scold me. And half the time she does not know whether it is me or Betsy, who is but a brat, that she scolds.

Martha is not, though, as free as she would like to think. She may have servants to wait on her, but she has to wait on her husband. She must serve him as a servant does her master. A girl indeed might be better off as a hired servant, since, whatever her station, she must work like such to some degree. If I were a hired servant I might at least be honest and be free to act like one, and not be hedged around with rules I am not versed in. I could be out and about in the world, quite independent, knowing when I had my time off and when I did not. I would enjoy some company apart from my own family that I have always lived with. Why, I declare a servant's life must indeed be better than mine.

Mr Hazlitt had no wish to watch me sweeping or dusting, he had little regard for housekeeping. When you were in his rooms, looking out on Staple Inn and removed from the din of the street with its traffic and the hawkers and sellers at their cries, you could forget what you were.

'Pray sit down on my knee,' he begged, in place of 'The fender needs polishing' or 'The shutter is gone askew, pray see to it', which is what you get from Mr Griffith or Mr Follett.

I ought not have made a habit of obliging, because here it was mid-morning and I still dressed in my morning-gown. Other than that I do not see why it should be so wrong, though he wrote it down as one of my crimes. Martha did say it was a habit engaged in only by kitchen-maids. But you can be sure she was not above sitting on Mr Roscoe's knee all the times they used to be closed in the parlour.

'It is not the same thing at all,' she declared in her stiff Mrs Roscoe manner.

'We are all pleased to fancy our behaviour is not the same as the common run,' I said. 'Well, I see no reason why it is not the same.'

When I sat on his lap he caressed me with a degree of intimacy I considered to be usual and not untoward in the circumstances. He gave off the clean odour of hard soap – he kept himself trim for me, I believe, though he did not always look it – and a faint scent of tobacco, to which I have no objection. He was not himself given to smoking pipes, but in the low places he frequents there is a great deal of smoking done and the fumes attached to him. My hair that he loosed from under my cap was at his disposal, and my bodice to undo. But nothing more, whatever he hints at, for that would be light – and I am not a light character.

It was curious to me to watch the flush deepen beneath his pallor until his face burned like a dull coal, and the severity of his expression fight with a softer emotion until it was overpowered. There was nothing to be heard except perhaps Betsy's step on the stairs and Baby calling to her. Hooting and hollering, 'Bethy, Bethy,' for he had a baby's lisp and could not yet say his esses. And now he will never learn to say them, poor little thing.

Well, why should I not be in his room, since it was a place I found agreeable? The fire I had laid was glowing at last and I had Mr Hazlitt hooped around me so you could think me the most interesting sight in the world. If his transports resulted in any greater attempts than fondling, you can be sure I would make to rise up in dismay. Then he would plead with me to stay.

'I will be good, Sarah, if you will only stay a little while.'

To make him promise to be good, I knew, was proper conduct. Then he would tell me his ideas on one subject or another. Is this to be held against me? That I took pleasure in his company? Is a girl to go off and marry the first man whose company she finds pleasure in? How else is a girl to find out whether she can love a man or not? Only by those means which both nature and society have designed for us – though the one is in general at odds with the other. To fix on someone, you must have a comparison, and then there is a proposition to be assessed.

Is a girl not entitled to make comparisons and assessments? I say she should be – but no, she is prevented by their sanctions. A man would be in fear for his pride if her decision did not go his way. In Mr Hazlitt's case he was not gallant enough to accept mine.

My pride was in many particulars flattered by him. That he chose to rehearse with me his books and his opinions, and that he had declared it was me and my admiration he was courting when he wrote. In consequence I often could not help remaining in his room to listen to him discourse until it was near dinner-time. Oh, the other lodgers might sleep in undressed beds and wash in yesterday's basins for all Mr Hazlitt cared. If it were Cajah and not I who was always in his room, and prepared to be under his influence, my father would have been better pleased. Father hoped – indeed, he hopes still – that Cajah would take up some course of study that would qualify him for a good position. He had hopes of making him a lawyer.

'You must settle to something,' he says. 'A man who is idle is a good-for-nothing.'

My mother is happy with Cajah whatever way he is and whatever he does. For the present at least, he is idle. He has notions of becoming a poet and competing with great men such as Lord Byron and Mr Wordsworth and can make up a line or two in an instant out of his head. Such as the one he invented in the kitchen once, when I would not give him argument on some subject, what he said was 'a paean to Sal'. 'Her brow unlined without, and too within/Unstrained by press of content 'gainst the skin . . .' I remember it because it was a dig at me and what he chose to present as my want of cleverness. But that is as far as he got. He wants the application to get beyond a couplet.

Cajah frequents the resorts, such as the Fives, where all the idlers of the town are to be found. Were it not for this habit of Cajah's I would know little of Mr Hazlitt's antics at the Fives. I would fancy him playing a quiet and able game there for exercise, and then tramping about the town, a solitary genius ruminating his words for the morrow, or consorting with great fellows like Mr Wordsworth and Mr Lamb in the fine houses of important gentlemen. I would not know he went about with a swearing dissipated set, racketing and gambling, with thieves and drunkards and fighting-men from the Seven Dials. Fancy that, when at home he could play such a lofty fellow. Oh, at the dinner-table Cajah could paint a most comical picture of Mr Hazlitt at his game of rackets.

'Who is that near-naked gentleman? Who, alone among them all, has whipped off his coat and weskit? Why, 'tis our dear Hazlitt. And who runs about in his shirt, stopping every minute to hitch up his breeches for the want of braces? Who else but Hazlitt? . . .' Here, my mother would be crying with laughing. And I too laughed, though it did not please me much to hear my friend ridiculed.

'And who is it who is bellowing like a bullock at the market when he is cornered? Why, Hazlitt's sighs and groans might be heard from the other end of Saint Martin's Lane. Then you can tell he is playing with a particular lack of success. We all line up to watch him, for he presents a comedy as fine as a show at the playhouse. Now he is stamping and roaring like a wounded beast, now he paces the court and glares about him as if to devour some poor spectator, only that he is hardly conscious we are there . . .

'Why, he's a perfect sport. When he misses a ball he wails and laments as if he had just seen off his whole family to Bottomless for thieving. He clutches his head in his hands when the ball deals him the smallest mishap, and when it is next contrary, is likely, if you are lucky, to make a run at the wall and dash his head against it. 'Tis a wonder he hasn't jellied his brains inside. And maybe he has, for he is wild enough and strange enough to allow you to think he has a jelly, and a French jelly at that, for the contents of his head. If by some chance he wins, he flings his racket full across the court – and look out, anyone up at the end, where it comes down. By this time he is drenched in sweat and his shirt is as sopping as if it was left to soak all night in a basin. You may wonder, Mother, where all the tea he drinks goes, but I do not, after seeing him at rackets. And what does he do next? He tears off his shirt and now he is almost naked, for his knee-breeches are falling down again and he has forgotten, or is too weary, to draw them up. And in a little while he is shivering with cold like a horse after it has bolted and he gathers up his weskit and coat from where they are lying in the dust of the floor and pulls them on over his wet pelt. I dare say he gives off a sweet fragrance by the time he comes home. What do you say, Sarah?'

With Father present, listening hard, I could see,

though he was silent, I thought it best look down at my plate and make no reply.

'A fellow told me this for a story,' went on Cajah. 'He left the Fives along with Hazlitt after one of these drenching displays of his. And when they had gone a little way, Hazlitt came to a stop in the middle of his speech. "You must not be seen walking with a man who has no shirt to his back," he announced. "Here we will part." '

'And what did the fellow do?' asked Betsy, her eyes very big.

'Why, the fellow considered it very considerate in him and was glad to be allowed to part.'

'I don't know but that I should be as glad to allow Mr Hazlitt to part from us,' my mother declared, wiping with her fists her eyes that were wet from laughing. But she did not mean it, as she was glad enough of his money and the good name he gave our house as a man of renown.

'We are proud to have Mr Hazlitt under our roof,' put in my father, in the stiff tone he has when he is ill-pleased. 'We should remember that he is a man whose natural passion and temperament must have an outlet for their expression even when he is away from the pressures of his writing-table.'

'That temperament of his expends all his force, for it is not to be found in him elsewhere,' grinned Cajah. 'You should see the puny little man he is when he is stripped to his bare chest on the courts.'

At this he gave me a direct and meaning look, which caused me to redden. But indeed I need not have, for I had never seen Mr Hazlitt bare-chested. And whatever I may think of him now it gave me no happiness to hear him ridiculed over the well-picked bones of mutton-chops while Betsy made messes with her fingers of the mashed turnip I had left on my plate and Baby lapped up like a puss the milk he had spilled in his.

'The women of the town are well received at the Fives,' said Cajah, unable to leave his own particular bone alone, 'for once the men have tired of their more public sports they like to pluck one beldam or another out of the flock, like a hen for the pot. Several among them are well known to Mr Hazlitt. They know him by his name and consort with him like old friends. I dare say there is a quantity of tin exchanged with more than a few of them.'

At this my father got up from his place with a warning show of clatter and coughs and withdrew to his chair by the fire.

Even my mother wanted no more stories from Cajah on that score. 'As long as there is no exchange in this house,' she said, 'a gentleman's acquaintance is his own business.' And she bade Betsy clear the table and me to see to the lights on the stairs, for evening was drawing down and the gentlemen would be soon come in. And Cajah, who is never bid do anything, sat on alone with his jug of beer – though deprived of an audience to attend to whatever else of import about Mr Hazlitt that he wished to impart.

I assisted Betsy in the dressing of her dolls until she went to bed. Tiring of that, she laid down Polly, who has the prettier face of the two, on the counterpane and placed two pennies, from the heap that she had been counting from her money-box, over her eyes. I considered it morbid in Betsy to represent a corpse.

'La, Bets, what has killed poor Polly?' I asked.

'She is not dead,' she chided me.

'Why, then, does she wear coppers on her eyes like a corpse?'

'That is Mr Hazlitt's money and it is what she sees in him.'

'Why?'

'You are a dunce, Sal. It is because she is a woman of the town.'

For a while I went about wondering to myself what my friend's conduct was with those fancy women, and if he sat them on his lap as he did me, and if it made them all atremble. Whether when I left him and his pleas and his self-pitying gaze, and he left the house, as he often did, soon after, and set off along the street with a quickened step, he was going to one or other of them, that she might give for a shilling what he did not wish to ask of me – for he well knew I would never give it – for love. I wondered if any of them could be as much a friend to him as I was. I was so much in the house that I had no knowledge of him outside it separate to the way he presented himself to me.

From the parlour window, when I put down my needle or my book, I could often observe him as he left the house and stepped out into the town. His gait was in general slow; he appeared burdened by age and thought. But having seen him contented in the morning, I fancied he went along now with a kind of swagger, vanishing into the vapours that were the same grey as that old frock-coat of his, his head raised as if he intended to accost the very sun itself and coax it from its hiding. Well, it is an excellent thing, I thought, to be a man with a man's independence and to pass an afternoon racketing and gambling on cock-fights at the Fives, after enjoying a kiss from the serving-maid in the morning.

A decent girl cannot go to the Fives to see the cocks or the fighting-men pound away at each other, unless she is happy to mix in with the women of the town. Well, I may as well daub my face with rouge and join them in the parade, for to any man's eye now I am no better. What use is it to plead I am better? All a girl can do is look to her character, and it is more fragile than a china teacup. Once it is broken, it cannot be made whole again. Though you persist in trying, it will still show wider a crack than any cup.

14

Mr Hazlitt liked to give me presents. They were nice presents, of his own choosing, and reflected, I thought, the honourable regard he had for me. I had from him volumes of his own hand – *Table Talk* when it came out and *Characters in Shakespeare's Plays*, which was older and covered in the same beautiful bindings as his *Political Essays*, the first of his books that he gave me. I found them uncommon vigorous. Why should I not accept them? They were not meaning presents. Why, anyone can read his books, only they must pay for them. They but signified that we were friends.

When I turned twenty on the eleventh of November, he gave me for a birthday present a prayer-book bound in crimson calf-leather.

'I am sure it is the nicest little book I ever saw,' I exclaimed, for the leather was so soft and rich-coloured and all so new. I have no objection to reciting my prayers, just as I like to recite my favourite verses – though I do not know that I belong in particular to any Church. We were taught to be Unitarian like my father, but in a small way, as my mother has little reverence for church or churchmen.

I had nothing from Mr Hazlitt yet for a Christmas present and wondered would I get something. He had told me he intended to pass the feast day in Wiltshire with his son. And sure enough, on the morning he was going off into that county, he took from a drawer, with a show of ceremony, a little package and presented it to me. On unwrapping the paper I found two small gold hearts, of the kind that hang on chains so you may carry them around your neck.

He showed me how the two halves of the heart flicked open with the help of a hinge. 'Do you see?' he said, smiling at my pleasure. 'There is room enough for a lock of hair to nestle in.' He requested of me that I stand so that he might cut a lock from my hair.

'Take but a little tendril, sir,' I said with a laugh, 'for I cannot spare a great deal.'

He promised to do as I asked and I stood for the knife.

'Now, Sarah, it is your turn to play Delilah,' he smiled.

So I took my turn with the paper-knife and sliced quite an ebony curl from his head. Then, his hair was yet black with but a few ribs of grey in it.

He placed with a tender care the severed locks of our hair in the little golden hearts. And then he secreted his in my bodice and I hung mine about his neck under his shirt. I know it could be said that this is the conduct of lovers. But as I saw it at the time, we more resembled two children who play at being serious, while they know well it is nothing more than a game. Why, the conduct of any gentleman is that of a child when he plays at love. To me it was harmless, because I did not mean by it what he meant and intended me to mean. And I had never got a locket before, as a child nor as a woman. How was I to tell that for him it represented a further link hammered home in his possession of me?

They were nice presents. I accepted them in the grateful manner they deserved. But I had no thought that I was investing promises in their acceptance. And now look what he does. He writes I am greedy for taking them and was fond and grateful to him only to get more presents from the same source in the future.

Indeed I am not such a poor creature as that. I may have no means of getting money for myself, but I might have a book from my father any day of the week, I am sure; I have only to ask for it. Only, I do not trouble him as it would be wasteful, when I can borrow whatever volumes I wish from the Roscoes.

As for the golden heart, I do not say I would have elected to have a curl from his head in it if I had a choice in the matter. And I do not see why his carrying a metallic heart around his neck should be regarded as his gaining possession of my real beating one. When your heart is your own you have no notion that a man may feel himself entitled to lay claim to it by carrying around its small dead likeness.

If I had been wise enough to attempt to refuse the books and the heart and the other presents he pressed on me later, I do not believe it could have been done. I knew what their refusal would bring on. He would engage me in a long enquiry as to my reasons for refusing them – which could have no other outcome after a tiresome taxing of my brains but the same one of acceptance. I was no match for him in argument. He was as effective at speech-making as Mr Brougham who got Queen Caroline off.

'We are not betrothed,' I might have said for an objection.

He would answer, 'Must we be betrothed for you to read what I have written?'

'Some people might think so.'

'You disappoint me, Sarah. That kind of scruple is surely for people other than we are.'

In this manner he would manage to chide me for the

commonplace nature of my scruples while pretending that he would never be so low as to have them himself. I had learned as early in our acquaintance as this to avoid the subject of love. If I were able to speak on the subject, I might have said, 'I cannot accept them because they are love-tokens.'

And he would demand, 'But do we not love one another, Sarah?'

'Not in the way they suggest, sir.'

'In what way, then, do you love?'

I would not have known how to answer, since I did not know my own mind or heart at that time and what I knew of love was cloudy. Also, there was the natural fear I had of giving him offence. And he would assume the pallor which expressed that he was angry and would take to pacing up and down, blinding me with a sophistry that let me know he was not ready to accept my plain-speaking.

I know now that there are many degrees of love, but there is only one that allows of possession. I was childish enough at that time, as I had but turned twenty, to accept his presents like a child from whom nothing is expected in return save a kiss.

'You have made me the happiest man alive,' he told me, his face lighting up to prove it.

Even had I admitted to myself that this was no everyday affection between a gentleman much advanced in age and intellect and a girl who would never think of regarding herself his equal, what could I have done in the face of his happiness? I pitied him, so wished contentment for him – and joy, also, seeing as it was seasonal. From Wiltshire he wrote me a letter that I considered somewhat extravagant in its expression of affection, but not untoward or wanting in sincerity. He told me he was tramping the roads around Winterslow and continued to write his book. And when he was not at his writing, he said, he was thinking of me. I sent him there the *London Magazine* as he had instructed. We did not see him again for several weeks.

15

Spring was opening when he came back to London. On his arriving home to us, he came direct downstairs and rapped on the kitchen door in search of me. When I was not to be found he told my mother that she was to be sure to send me up with his tray in the morning. Then he went out and she saw no more of him.

It was an evening I was visiting at the Roscoes. My niece was growing bigger now and was more agreeable. She would smile if you coaxed her and was less given to the crying fits she was used to. But she and Baby between them had driven me to think I would not like to be charged with bringing an infant into the world with all their discontents and pains that they seem to be more conscious of than we are.

'I am resolved not to marry,' I told Martha. 'Besides, I would not like to belong to a man and be a slavey in his house while he goes about as he pleases and returns only when he wants his comforts.'

'It may please you to speak like a Woolly' – which is what she calls the followers of Miss Wollstonecraft – 'but you are likely to regret it,' she said. 'It can only benefit a lady to be grateful for her inferiority. And if she does not feel it, well, she can affect it. Her husband then will be gratified and will love her all the more.'

The love of Mr Roscoe had made her better than content, she said, and such a love as his was as much as any girl needs. 'In any case, you will hardly escape it,' she said. 'If you were plain you might.'

'I am plain,' I protested. 'My eyes want colour.'

'They will do, since your other features are pretty enough.'

She told me that if I ate more esculents, and did not confine myself to picking at my bread and milk, their colour would deepen. I was repelled by the prospect but agreed to try.

Well, the fields and woods and fresh air and whatever else of good they enjoy in the country had wrought no great change in Mr Hazlitt; he looked the same as ever he did. His rooms too were as he had left them, as you can be sure not one of us had mounted that far to dust or sweep while he was absent. My greeting was no less warm than his, but I felt myself shy from not seeing him for so long and to hide my blushes was glad to have the place to set to rights.

As I went about my work I heard him sigh on occasion and knew his gaze was bent on me, as if he sought to know whether there was any change in me and perhaps any change in his affection for me.

'Did you miss me, Sarah?' he enquired at last.

'I did, sir, a little,' I answered.

'What did you miss?'

'Our conversations.'

'And our caresses?'

'A little also, sir.'

I like to tell the truth when I can. And it was true that I had been more listless and dismal than I was used to since Christmas was past. I had no means of amusement or none that did not appear staled or tame, and went about mired in days so dark and foggy you could fancy life an endless night. I had the sensation sometimes, and it was not comfortable, that I was little more than a ghost or a phantom. A phantom sent to fetch the beer from the Old Serjeant, a shade going from one shadowy shop to another, a pale spirit wandering unseen among the passengers in the vaporous streets and in the muddy parks among the black and twisted trees.

Mr Hazlitt begged me then to take my old seat on his lap. And like a ghost I did – though one that might be human again if she were plied with enough heat and solicitudes.

Now we were together again after so long apart, he was more pressing than he was wont and his touch was more urgent than it should be. Alarmed by my weakness in the face of it, I withdrew to the door as if on the point of going, that he might cool. I had no wish to leave him as I had been much on my own. But I saw it was not in my interest to stay if he intended to be as peremptory with me as he might be with some woman of the town. He pleaded with me not to leave him, and succeeded in reassuring me when he said that he had been transported by seeing me again after he was away so long, and this transport was increased all the more by my proximity. I consented to stay, if it were at a distance. He said he would ask for nothing more.

'There you are, a dear apparition made flesh,' he marvelled. 'You cannot know how often I used to picture you these weeks past as you are now in your little mob-cap and morning-gown.'

Perhaps remarking my reluctance to hear such talk, he left off and spoke of the man Hunt, whose friend he was, and whose trial was going on then, for he was accused of sedition. It was to attend Mr Hunt's trial that he came up to London. During his discourse I was thinking with some amusement that I might have been taken in by his flattery. If the trial were not taking place he would not have come up at all but would be quite happy to go on only thinking of me – and out of my morning-gown, I supposed, as much as in it. But, seeing as he was coming up to town, he might as well enjoy the opportunity of fondling his Sally too.

'Poor Hunt will not get justice,' he asserted, 'for there is no such thing as justice in England.'

Here he produced a whole string of complaints and criticisms directed at everything that is English. I shall not rehearse them, for there is nothing more tedious than to go over an old treatise when you don't share the arguments of it. He has written down his complaints anyway against England and I shall only say that he spoke with the same fierceness, only more, that he wrote. Whether England is so much worse for injustice and corruption than is France, which he admires as though it were a paradise by comparison, I can't say. I have never journeyed as far as France.

However, I cannot imagine why it should be better. The mob may be better at getting its way there, certainly. But French fowls are puny articles and their legs of mutton too are smaller and not as sweet, at least my mother says so, and I have never heard anyone to disagree with her. Elegant folk may like to talk the French language, but I do not know why they should go to the trouble of trying to get their tongues about it. France is only good, as far as I can see, for keeping England fed – though not very well. I believe that is as much as you can say for it. And it could not have gone easier for Mr Hunt had he committed his treason there, as he got only a year in Coldbath Fields – though Mr Hazlitt was carrying on as if he were sentenced to swing.

It is my opinion that Mr Hazlitt is prejudiced against the English, for the reason that he is hardly English at all. He is after all half an Irishman. His father was Irish, from a little hamlet in the county of Tipperary. He told me the name, though now I forget it, but it struck me at the time that it must be near as wild and rude as Africa, from the sound of it. It is true that he can speak and write as good as any Englishman, and he did not appear to be so foolish as to be proud of his Irish connections, though he did not hide them either. And he never professed any love or attachment for that rough country and its miserable people. However, they do not like us any more than we like them, so I suppose his contempt for England is only what comes natural to an Irishman and he cannot help it.

Cajah used to say that, as Mr Hazlitt was an old Jack, he would like us all to rise up and murder the King, while he directed our acts of treason to his satisfaction from the King's own throne. But it is my opinion that, seeing as he cannot claim to love Ireland if he does not wish to be a laughing-stock, he chooses France for a country to admire instead. He wants an opposition to England and France will do − in particular since it is a vast and populous place, I dare say, and more profitable to praise in the magazines for a fee.

One of his fancies was that I should travel with him there, and thence as far as Italy. I own that I half-fancied the proposition in part and dreamed for a while, in an idle way, of going. It cannot be a great distance, as there are ships and barques of all kinds that set out every day.

'We might travel in the new steamship,' he said, 'that crosses the channel in under three hours. Would you ever consider that proposal, Sarah?'

I would agree to nothing, since I do not like to make rash promises as men do. And in any case I would not wish him to consider me light for accepting too ready.

'If I were free . . . Might you come then?' he asked, thinking he understood why I was silent.

'I could never consent to run off with a man,' I told him.

Although indeed a girl can run off and come to no

harm in the end if she is sure of the man. But it was the right answer to give Mr Hazlitt.

'I am glad to know you would not, Sarah,' he said, with a meaning look.

I was but a girl then, and I own I was not above day-dreaming of the proposition on occasion, in particular when London looked especial drear. Now I am a woman of twenty-and-three and I would not consent to go down the street with him, let alone to France.

In those days it could please me, the prospect of leaving London behind. You can suffer the headache here from morning till night on account of all the din – unless you are fortunate and have your rooms to the back, as Mr Hazlitt did. There is the shrieking of the nags and the rattle of their shackles, and the rumblings and creaks of every degree from carts and carriages and the clatter of their iron wheels on the cobbles. And all the shouts and cries, for the costers are never done bawling for their pennies. They have hardly sold you the wherewithal for dinner before they are calling out their wares for supper. There are people crowded and cramped everywhere, and more and more coming in on top of us every week, they do say. And I can well believe it, because any day you venture out there is a mass of new faces to be seen, if you had a mind to observe them, as grey and pinched as the sky we go about in general under, or looming up an inch from your nose when the fog is down.

It pleased me to fancy the Continent a smaller place – and brighter. Indeed, I am sure it cannot have a city the size of London, for it is well known that London is the greatest city in the world. And I think that in a land where there is a baking sun in all seasons the people must wear a lighter and brighter costume than ours. Also, as they speak a different tongue, there can be no point in conversing with them. For this reason I fancy it to be a near noiseless place where, seeing as it would make not an iota of sense to me in any case, the din might all be at a pleasant remove. I fancy that to live there would be like living in the peace of an apartment to the back – one equipped with great windows that look out at the same time on to the street, so that you may watch the doings and the to-and-fro but are never called upon to speak, and know what is going forward while you remain on your balcony at home.

Mr Hazlitt's projection of the steamship, I own I was drawn to. Martha declared she would never consent to go in such a thing that went along puffing and blowing, not until it was well proved and she could be sure it would not founder. But I am sure there is not a vessel made that is guaranteed never to founder.

Not, indeed, that I ever let her know I might entertain the notion of crossing the sea in the steamship with Mr Hazlitt, but presented it as just another remarkable thing I heard they had invented. I was sure she would be grievous worried by the degree of intimacy that had sprung up between myself and Mr Hazlitt. From the way in which Mr Roscoe and his friends spoke of him, she thought him a fierce and awesome fellow and certainly too elderly to be considered.

I do own I may have been a little troubled myself by his proposal, though I was hardly conscious enough of it to square up to it. I expect I should have known better. After all, what drew me to him was the impression he gave of sincerity. He put on none of the false notes a man does when he wants the use of you in his room but has no serious attachment.

And yet in the end he was no better than such a man, because his understanding of me was no better than that of a fellow who never troubles himself to attempt it. I would have done just as well to sit with any one of them, Mr Griffith or Mr Follett or Mr Bellew, if it was sympathy or understanding I wanted. And I dare say that must be what any girl wants. Mr Hazlitt was false to himself as well as to me. He loved only what he had conjured up out of his fancy.

'Come and see what I have here, Sarah,' he greeted me one morning. More jaunty than he was used to be, he drew me with a great show of excitement to the wall opposite his writing-table. Here he had hung up a picture. 'Now I may feast upon your image in my own time as much as in yours,' he declared.

The girl represented in the picture he considered to be the exact image of me, and had purchased it in consequence. I suppose he came upon it in one of the dusty old shops in Wych Street.

The background was very pretty, for it shone out, being gold. But I did not like to accept that the creature depicted was my likeness. She wore quite a melancholy expression. She was a saint, he believed. One caught in a condition of extreme suffering, I thought, such as a martyr is, or besieged by some malevolence. It was this sad saintly personage he was enraptured with, who had little to do with the living one that I was. He would be made happy, I am sure, if I were never to smile. Well, there are men who prefer to kiss ideal images and he is one of them.

On another morning, he showed me in a book a drawing of a marble statue and declared its limbs were replicated in mine. But he was never privy to my limbs. He may have caressed them on occasion, but I do not believe I ever revealed them so he might study them and find a resemblance. Never, at least, in their entirety. He would have had to watch me through the keyhole as I undressed if he were to know them as well as that.

16

However, he had perhaps greater justification than I was ready to admit when he compared me to his sad saint, for I confess I was much inclined to melancholy in those months.

What occurred in our house in the March of the year I do not wish any more to dwell on, though there was a long while when I could not cease from dwelling on it. After all, there is hardly a house in town or country that does not know such a misfortune, and often a house knows several, one following upon another. We are indeed to be considered fortunate that we had to face it in ours only the once. It is an everyday occurrence, and what good can it do anybody to dwell on it or wonder at it? But you can hardly help it when it comes to your own little brother, and he still only a totterer. And all the more when you were used to regarding him as little better than a nuisance. And did not love him as you might, but teased him, and smacked him when he would not keep from climbing the stairs, even if it was for his own good.

Baby was prone to attacks of the smatticks ever since he was born. That winter he was often ill with the cough and had the whoop quite bad after Christmas. But the weather was now growing milder and that day he seemed to be faring a great deal better. Mr Hazlitt was absent again, but we had a new lodger, Mr Bulrose, who came to us through Mr Follett, so Baby was put out to play in the yard. We had such a lot of work to do, in particular as my mother took a fit and put Betsy and me to clean, now that spring was come, what we never touched in the regular course. And Baby could not be kept from mischief, without Betsy to watch him, if he was indoors. I threw out his ball to him to keep him amused. And he had his pair of tin soldiers that Father had made up little coats for, the small one dressed in blue to represent the French colours, and the tall one in scarlet for ours, with the ittiest of tin buttons attached to each, so he could dress and undress them as he pleased.

When it grew chill he was busy making pies in the mud and would not consent to come in when I was sent to fetch him. However, I remarked he was in the kitchen some time after dinner was cleared away. By nightfall, when Mother at last had a moment to look at him, she found he was hot with a fever. She was anxious and tried to make him take some supper. But he turned away from any food or drink except for some sugared milk. The following day he was worse. 'He might have as much barley-sugar as he wishes if he would only take it,' cried Mother. But he was not to eat a bit of anything ever again.

It was not an easy matter either to get him to take his physic. My mother was only able to persuade him to take a little of the sudorific that was always kept by for him. We thought of asking the Welshman Mr Griffith, who is an apothecary, to come down, but Mother does not like to disturb the lodgers with kitchen matters. And in any case, she prefers Mr Mellett from the Strand for an apothecary. He was sent for and came prompt enough. He took his pulse and declared it was much accelerated. He looked quite grave, which alarmed us all, and bled poor Baby.

Father came home and found us all in such a worried state of mind there was no supper ready for him. We had been capable only of the preparation of a succession of fresh possets for the little invalid in the hope that he might agree to swallow one of them. But Father was soon as grave and anxious as we were and could not muster any appetite for a dish of braised beef fetched from the chop-house, though it was always his favourite.

Next, on Father's instructions, Mr Armstrong, the physician from Covent Garden, was sent for. He appeared more hopeful. He placed blisters on Baby's spine and at his ears and prescribed antimony. But that was of no use as he could not take it. I do not believe physic ever is of any use. But you must go and fetch it anyway, for there is nothing else you can do in such a circumstance that might furnish a glimmer of hope. The cough continued, a sore and racking one. He was not quiet from it until it came the sixth of March and he left us. Before he did, he turned his lilac-tinted face to Betsy, who had been used to serve as his mother, even if often not a very good one.

'Bethy? Do you say I will die?' he demanded.

His voice was shocking, as it was a new one for him, and hoarse. He had never spoken more than as a baby and she got a great fright. This was the last look he gave and they were the last words he spoke.

My mother took care not to trouble nor neglect her lodgers at least, so they knew little of Baby — indeed, I fancy some among them hardly knew he had ever lived — lying so sick in his cot by the kitchen fire that was kept heaped up whether he was icy or burning with the fever. Now, here was Betsy running mad about the house, weeping and shrieking. 'He is gone so cold.

He is gone so cold,' she was crying out, and would not give up. It was merciful that this took place in the afternoon and we were alone in the house. And it is a blessing Mr Hazlitt was absent or I believe he might have joined in the shrieking, for he is so liable to a phrensy himself.

Betsy was sent to stay with the Roscoes where there was the other babe, her niece Emma, to play with and where she need not see Baby gone all cold anymore. And I was given leave to put off attending to the lodgers for some days, which was a blessing too, on account of my heavy and bleary eye and red and swollen looks. Lizzie's niece, who is a big country girl, came from the cottage in Putney and took charge of the gentlemen in place of us.

Baby John was but three years of age and had a beaming smile when he chose to display it – though in general he wore the smug pout that an infant does when it thinks itself the most important personage in the world and is happy with its lot. He was just starting to be a healthy and pudgy boy when he was took.

On the day following that sad one, for there was no reason to delay it any further, there were the mutes at the door with their muffled standards. Then we had the long mournful walk in our grim funereal cloaks behind the miniature coffin as far as Bunhill Fields. I wish we might have risen to a coach and plumed pair to carry him there, for Baby was so very fond of horses. But such a show as that would cost us thirty or forty pounds and the little fellow could not be sensible of it, were it as fine itself as a king's procession, it would be a silly expense to go to.

For quite a time I could not be rid of the sensation of horror I knew when I laid my hand on his small forehead and found it turned more cold and stony than

the marble tombs in Lincoln's Inn. I dare say I looked
melancholy enough to sit for any picture when next I
saw Mr Hazlitt.

17

'You look a little unwell, Sarah,' he remarked.

As he had been out of town, our small tragedy below stairs had passed him by. When I told him the baby had sickened and was buried, he was tender in his reply, murmuring he was sorry indeed for us. He said that when he came upon Baby playing at the bottom of the stairs, he had been glad to pat his fair little head. He spoke then with a moving affection of his own infants who had died and of William, the one remaining to him, who he had found to be a strong, robust boy when he last saw him in the country. But he was not keen to dwell on these matters relating to his former domestic life – in case, I suppose, though I thought nothing of it at the time, that I should be discouraged from regarding him in the light of an eligible.

Instead he led me to his easy-chair and before I knew it he had pulled me on to his lap. I dare say I was in want of comfort and a respite from my sad musings. I was so very weary of being below in the kitchen gloom, where my mother and Lizzie were lifting their aprons to their wet eyes with every heavy step they took. And, indeed, near to being overturned myself from the sick-pastilles that filled the air from their burners, intended for a freshener, but serving better as a grim reminder to us of death's stony countenance. In consequence I was open to Mr Hazlitt's attentions. I own I allowed him now to take fresh liberties.

He held me so close, and was so heated and quickened, I fancied we might be melded together. As well as kissing and fondling me with more freedom than I ever allowed him before, he felt secret parts of my person under my gown as he would if I were a wanton or a wife. I cannot say why I did, but at this I fell to weeping. But without making a din, such as Betsy makes, and my face buried in his neck so I am sure he did not know it.

This was not because what Mr Hazlitt was doing with me felt like wrongdoing. No, that came quite natural – but, then, I fear I may not be a good girl. No, perhaps indeed I cannot be, to have made Mr Hazlitt first love me and now to hate me as he does. His touch was not soft nor wandering. It was not calculated. He is not a sensual character, but intellectual and forceful and his touch was passionate. And if I am evil to have allowed it, then nature itself is evil. Well, if it is so, every action of ours, no matter how small or slight, must be said to be evil – as what are we at base but creatures of nature? But it cannot be so, for then we need have no scruples about anything, nor trouble ourselves as to whether an action, be it murder itself, is good or bad, only carry on like creatures who are devoid of any.

However, though I had no sensation in the world of evil I soon felt an alarm of imminent peril. I was practically gone away in a swoon, but just in time I stood up and placed myself at a distance, and smoothed down my slackened clothes. My fear was not of bringing a sin on my head, but ruin. My father and mother, though they might be happy to welcome another little John to replace the one we had lost, would not wish it, you can be sure, that he should come from me.

On that occasion Mr Hazlitt might well have forced himself upon me. He might have led me to his bed, that was still tumbled as I had got no further with my work than attending him at his breakfast. He might have had his way. Indeed, he advises the world in his book that there was many a time he could have had his way with me and he regrets he did not. After all, I did act like a light character who accepted his roving hands, on that occasion anyway, without any rebuke or fuss.

Maybe it was then, seeing my high emotion and contorted face, that he conceived the ambition to make me his wife rather than enjoy me as I came, and to be turned off when he wished. Proud as he is of course, he assumed I would have a natural gratitude that so very great and superior a personage as he should favour me with such an honour.

18

In a little while, the sorrow for the loss of my little brother was fading. After all, there was little to be gained by moping, as he could not be made by it to come back to us. And my former good sense was quicker yet to return. I made efforts to restore my friendship with Mr Hazlitt to its old footing, standing apart from him when we conversed and quitting the room if his endearments became too ardent or his kisses more than mild.

You may say I could have refused even that degree of attention. But what girl can hope to escape the attentions of a man who has set first his eyes, and then his heart, on her? Only by going off to a distant street where he cannot waylay her, and trusting that in a month or two she will slide out of his thoughts and be replaced by another. This escape was hardly open to me even had I known the prudence of it. Where was I to go? To live with my sister and her husband as if he were the poet Shelley and we his mistresses? No, I was a respectable girl, and my only place was in my father's house. And that place was to see to the lodgers, of which Mr Hazlitt was but one. Indeed, I cannot but think that it was a great mistake in me to make a show of prudence, from the point of view of my extrication. It was after this he began to speak of marriage.

I had laid out his breakfast-table and stood by his side as usual to keep him company. And, as usual, I was taking care to stand outside his reach. The morning sun, shining down for once, was making play with the wind and causing the rug, which was our best on account of gracing Mr Hazlitt's room, to dance with light like a carpet of gems. I was near about as content as I could be, just then. We had been mangled, but now we were getting over our troubles – why, even Mother had given up her weeping. I began to think the house could be its old self again, what with a summer, and its capacity to hunt off the glooms, on its way. I was given to falling into an idle fancy that there was some perfect gentleman, as I am sure any girl dreams up in that season, waiting for me who I was yet to meet. You see, already I was conjecturing him up, though I knew nothing yet of Henry being in the world.

Mr Hazlitt's toast was spread thick with butter as he likes it, but he left it unbitten on his plate and took only draughts from his cup. He was silent. He lifted the tea-kettle and made to pour from it and then put it down again as if he could not remember why he took up such a thing.

'Sarah,' he said, of a sudden. 'I wish to ask . . .' He did not continue.

'Shall I pour for you, sir?' I had the notion he had a sentimental wish to be served by my hand.

'I wish to ask . . .' His voice was congested. 'I wish to ask whether you will be my wife.'

He did not look at me but into the fire that was leaping up in the grate, a thing it would often not consent to do when it was most required.

'But you are married, sir,' I replied. In mentioning this impediment, which was plain as a pikestaff, I was

85

contented that I must be safe from any further discussion of the matter. I supposed he made his offer as a jest or hoped to reassure his self-esteem by hearing me make my assent.

'But if I were free,' he persisted, 'would you agree to be my wife?'

As he was not free, I had no concern in the matter and replied with a degree of carelessness I am very sorry for. 'I am sure I would, sir. But since you are not, there can be no use in talking of it.'

He leapt up from his seat and pressed me to him with a sincerity of feeling that frightened me. His next declaration frightened me more. 'I intend to get a divorce, Sarah. A divorce is a thing easy enough got in Scotland. And then we shall be married, and with as much legality as shall please you, and your father and the government of England itself could ask for.'

He was laughing now, and half-crying too, in the intemperate manner he could take on all of a sudden, and was showering kisses on my forehead and my head and declaring he was happy fit to burst, and that it was I who had put him into this joyous condition. Happiness, he declared, was a state that had ever escaped him and he had been sure it always would – until I had made my appearance in his life. I was the light of his days and the joy of his heart and he had never known anyone before to match me and never would again, he was sure, though he lived to be a hundred. But now since I had consented to marry him he never would have to seek my match. I was the sweetest maid in the whole world, whether in heaven itself or on the earth, according to him.

He was in such a transport that I was struck by his madness and was almost going along with it too – although not to the degree, I am sure, that I considered him the sweetest man ever to walk in the world. But I was dazed and thought every other moment that indeed we were to be married.

Then I came to myself and attempted to bring reason back into his talk and put forward arguments as to why such a thing was impossible. His wife, I protested, would surely not consent to be divorced.

This he waved aside as of no consequence. 'Our union was never one that either of us expected a great deal from. It suited Sarah to take a husband at the time and me to take a wife. It was in the nature of little more than a business arrangement for both of us.'

'Your wife too is called Sarah?' I was astonished by this coincidence, and thought it unfortunate, though I could not say why, as there must be near as many Sarahs in the world as there are Marys.

'There are a great number of Sarahs walking about, my angel. But to me you are the first Sarah and will be the only one too as soon as it can be managed . . .

'We suited one another quite well, that other Sarah and I,' he went on. 'In the way of people pleased to have a companion to share a scrag-end of mutton with and a bed when the fire dies down. She is a good woman and I am grateful to her for the gift of little William, our son. But she is a prosaic and commonsens- ical creature, and is reasonable enough to be the first to admit it. She was never able to incite love or tenderness in me as you do, my own dear darling Sarah, with your tender looks and your speaking ways.'

He was now pacing about the room and pouring out these words like an orator, who has a passionate need to persuade his audience and has every confidence, into the bargain, that he will. Thus, I suppose, are all men used to talking of their wives when they are hoping to persuade a girl into their bed. But I knew with a flurry of alarm that Mr Hazlitt was quite sincere. Coming up to where I stood stricken and flustered, though I believe I did not show it, he pressed me to him.

'Do you know that you have delivered me?' he murmured. 'You have made me a man, an ordinary miraculous happy man, such as I had given up all hope of being. You are an angel, sent to deliver me from my idiocies. And you shall be my own angel just as soon as I can manage it.'

He had the appearance indeed of having been delivered. His countenance was flushed, and his eyes were shining with an excess of damp in place of the brooding glow like a low-banked fire I was more used to.

'Do let me go, sir,' I pleaded, seeking to release myself from his arms.

'But you have often stayed longer with me,' he protested. 'And surely now, after what is agreed between us, you have every entitlement to stay.'

'I must go, sir' I repeated. For I feared I might suffocate, he was clasping me so tight.

'Let us have no more of that "sir" of yours,' he chided, while letting me go. 'Shall you not call me William, now we are betrothed?' His manner was joyful. 'I should like to hear you call me by my name. And it shall be Will or Willie as you wish, by and by.'

I got away and went up to my room and changed out of my morning-gown. In such a state was I at the turn things had taken that I put on my shawl and slipped out before anyone could mark my agitation. I set off in the direction of the gardens, though there was a great whirl of equinoctial wind flinging itself about, and me with it, making it not the best day for walking out. The air was fresh at least, with the sweetness that it has when it comes off the Channel, and cooling to my head. My gaze was bent on the dancing path beneath me so I'm sure no one could have told it, but my mind was in as much of a flurry and my thoughts skittering about like the tender leaves above my head.

I was impressed indeed that such a great man, as the public and my father regarded him, should appreciate me to the degree that he could see me in the light of a wife. I thought I could not be so insignificant after all. If Mr Bradley would not have me for his wife, well, another gentleman, not so well placed in the world but better admired by it, would.

So pleased was I by this that I even fancied I might accept his offer. And then I pictured my life as it would be with Mr Hazlitt and that was a thing I own I was not over-impressed with. It was by no means hateful to me, but neither did it seem sufficient to give up my home for.

In any case he could not mean it, I thought then as a comfort. And, after all, it was a long way off, for he had not spoken of setting out for Scotland on the morrow or the next day. And he would soon forget it or be sorry he ever proposed it.

I wondered what his friends, such as Mr Lamb, would say when they learnt of it. They would pay him no heed, I decided, and tell one another he was hot-headed and would soon repent of his folly – only, he must not delay or it would be too late and I would have him snared. As for me, my pride might be hurt a little when he repented, but I would not be so very disappointed at losing my chance to become Mrs Hazlitt.

My thoughts were confused by my natural gratitude to him for having solicited and honoured me to such a degree – but I should be just as grateful if, having done so, he would let me go. A girl in my position learns very early the ways of men. I believe ladies do also, but they pretend they do not. Then they can appear helpless and are not called upon to make any decisions that might hinder the men in whatever they intend. I concluded I was being foolish and acting the lady, and was wrong to listen to him at all, and it was all no more than a plot he had invented to persuade me into his bed. I went home less happy but more at ease.

I made no promise to marry Mr Hazlitt. But neither, I fear, did I speak plain enough to persuade him I would not. I thought I could not endure the scene I fancied he would produce if I went against him. It had not yet been directed at me, but I had a notion of the wildness of his temperament and his contempt. A man of sudden passions as he was, I was sure his feeling for me would soon blow over. I comforted myself that a man's heart is divided into compartments, like a dressing-chest, and some greater person than myself would come to fill my allotted space before very long. Indeed, even if it had been my greatest desire, I do not believe I would have placed any hope in his continuing in the wish to marry me. Our relation was all confined to his chambers, his courting and his certainties, and I thought that since it was contained there it must die down, as even the hungriest fire does, in time.

One thing I resolved was that my family must know nothing of his proposal. They might be alarmed by Mr Hazlitt's great age, and his wife that was yet living, and be cross that I had encouraged him to the degree suggested by a proposal. On the other hand, they might be glad enough of the honour. I had no wish to be under pressure from yet another quarter.

So I did not tell them. It was only Betsy I told, since we were so much together. She was clinging to me like an oyster to its shell since Baby's going and in consequence I was both her protector and playmate, though I often wearied of being either. After all, we slept in the bed together, so it was only natural, if unwise, that I should be rash sometimes in my confidences with her. While she brushed out my hair and I hers every night before the pier-glass, we had laughs at the expense of the lodgers, how this one left out his boots, and that one coughed thrice before requesting a service.

'Fancy, Bets, Mr Hazlitt has proposed that we be married,' I told her as she unloosed my hair.

On hearing of this new boldness in him, she declared it was only to be expected that he should wish to marry me.

'You have such pretty hair, Sal,' she remarked, spreading it dainty over my shoulders, 'and you walk so graceful, as if you did not involve your feet in the action, like the rest of us.'

She considered Mr Hazlitt to be not a bad man, though rather fearsome. 'He is always deep in his great thoughts and he greets me only seldom when I pass him on the stairs. And he is old and cannot live long and then you will be a widow and be obliged to wear black. And you do not suit black, Sarah, I believe, though you are handsome in your white muslin.'

'You cannot say I am handsome,' I told her, 'whether in black or white. A man is said to be handsome. A girl is said to be pretty.'

'A lady too can be said to be handsome.'

'I am not one of them.'

'Your eyes are not pretty, Sarah. But they might be called handsome.'

I found that impudent in her and I told her she was to get into bed and leave me the candle as I wished to read my book.

'But your eyes hardly let you read in daylight, let alone with a candle,' she protested.

'I can read as well as anyone.'

She would not let me alone but sat hunkered on the bed. 'Do you consider Mr Hazlitt to be handsome?' she asked my reflection in the glass.

I replied that I did not think him plain. 'Do you think him handsome?' I could not forbear asking. 'I suppose you would call him pretty?'

'His looks are uncommon,' she said, grave as a parson. 'But he is not pretty enough for you to marry – I would not marry him. Though, indeed, you are not so pretty yourself . . .' At this she burst out laughing like a young horse whinnying in the way she does.

In a little while, when she was lying in bed, her hair tucked under her cap, she asked, 'Has Mr Hazlitt kissed you?'

'He has not.'

She frowned. 'A gentleman must kiss you when he makes you an offer.'

'Only when you accept the offer.'

'I will marry a gentleman,' she mused. 'But one younger and better-sized than Mr Hazlitt. And I will kiss him only when we have a baby, but after that whenever I want.'

I turned her my back.

'Will you not kiss me good night, Sarah?' she pleaded.

I made no answer.

'It is an excellent thing that Mr Hazlitt should wish to marry you,' she remarked after a little in her placating way. 'It shows you are pretty and all the gentlemen will be making you their offers.'

'He considers me as pretty as any angel.'

'Well, then, so you must be. And if you accept him I will go to call on you and will keep you company when he is at the Fives.'

'If you must kiss me, you may,' I told her, now that I was mollified.

'I am sorry, Sarah, for insisting on it, but I must. Else I am sure I will have the nightmare.'

She kissed me and was grateful for it, and next thing she was asleep.

I thought this was how it might be to lie with Mr Hazlitt. He full of his own thoughts and doings like Betsy, and I fond of him as of her – but hardly more. And he would not sleep as ready as she, but would turn to me and want more than a kiss and to enjoy me as a wife. The prospect was not so terrible and made me fear I might be in danger of accepting his proposal, even if I would prefer to avoid it.

19

As the days passed, I took little pleasure in thinking I was a girl who might be affianced if she wished and put all thought of it aside. Mr Hazlitt spoke no more about his divorce and I supposed he had forgotten it. He still insisted on his morning kiss and in general I gave it – though sometimes I did not, being more in danger than I wished to be when I did, and fearing to get myself into a scrape. I was sure it was best to keep a distance between us, but this was not easy as we had reached a pitch of intimacy before. A girl should know that this is a condition it is not too easy to draw back from.

The spring had passed slow for everyone, whether they had lost someone to it or no, as the days continued cold and wet until we were all heartily sick of it. Our house had been sunk especial low in spirits. And we were going about in the same tired old heavy drab for such a long time and my winter shawl was grown shabby and burdensome like a skin that refused to be shed. I hardly ventured out except to fetch what was necessary for the table. Even dining had lost its taste for the rest of them due to sorrow and sameness and much of the day's victuals went to fill the swill-cart. I dare say the swine in Putney at least were happy.

Then one day all of a sudden it was summer, so you

could not mistake it. The house was comfortable as a warming-oven, and my mother bade the windows to be flung open, admitting all the stifling smells and miasmas the heat brings – though, no matter, the airing was welcome for all that.

'You may buy a box of mignonette,' she told me, 'if you see one going about. I do not think Baby would hold it against us to be gay.'

Before going up to see to Mr Hazlitt, I put on my short-sleeved muslin that was mended and washed some weeks past to be ready for its outing on such a day.

'Well, the maids can don their summer-gowns at last,' he said, which was a remark my father could make just as easy and cheerful, or Mr Griffith.

By and by, as he took his tea, holding my hand all the while, he grew more sentimental. 'Is that not the gown you wore, Sarah, when I first laid eyes upon you? You glided towards me in that way of yours and I was lost as I never was. I loved you then. Well, I adore you now.'

He caressed my arm. They are thin, my arms, but at least they are smooth, and white too.

'I always like to see a girl in simple dress. Although she, I know, may like a touch of splendour. When you are my wife you shall have as many splendid gowns as you choose in the finest French style. You shall wear crimsons and purples and emerald-greens and any colour of the rainbow that pleases you. They will go only to show you off as the heroine of a romance that you are.'

Before, I might have answered him light, but now I was uneasy because he had brought up the subject of our marriage, when I hoped he had forgotten it, or recognised it for the folly it was. I was silent. Taking this for timidity and acquiescence with his sentimental mood, he drew me on to his lap. Soon he was breathing hard and was pressed warm and close against me. I could hear his heart through the thin stuff of his shirt and he placed my fingers on his chest so I could feel how it beat.

I did not intend it – indeed, it was against my wishes – but I was touched and let him make a little free with me as he wished. And now it was he who pulled back, exclaiming that he would never stoop to take advantage of so good and sweet a girl as I was.

Well, I was thankful, as any girl should be. But if he had taken advantage that might have put an end to it, for he could hardly wish for such a girl as a wife, and surely that would have been for the best.

I did not go near him for some days, so confused was I by my own conduct as much as I was by his, but obliged Lizzie to see to him and to tell him I had the gripes. Until I heard his steps on the stairs that signified he was quitting us for the day, I stayed out of sight in the kitchen or at a distance from his rooms. Often he would hesitate, as if he was about to come looking for me, and twice he tapped on the parlour door when I was inside. I made no reply. Once he was gone out I need not fear the prospect of running into him for the rest of the day.

But in a while I tired of my own company and missed my morning talks. And also mother was complaining of me slinking about and being idle, while Lizzie grumbled that she had enough to do in the kitchen without mounting the stairs as well. So I went back to my old ways. Well, I thought, to excuse myself, he will know now the kind of a girl I am and will have put aside his fine notions that I am suitable for a wife. At the same time I decided to resist him better than I had before. I came into his room, determined to be good but pleasing, and as if nothing had happened between us.

I could not have been more mistaken. He was full of joy at seeing me again.

'My dear one, how anxious I was to hear you were ill . . .' He inspected my countenance, very anxious to see how I was. 'You are better, I see, though yet a little pale. But after all, my Sarah is always pale . . .'

Distracted, he darted this way and that, presenting a book to me that he hoped I would like, and taking it from me again as I made to open it; beating a cushion for me and, before I had a chance to sit, sitting down on it himself. He reached out for my hand. I gave it to him but continued to stand at a fair distance.

'I have been busy, Sarah, about our business,' he burst out, eager as a barrow-boy. 'And find that things are not as simple as they should be. We do not as yet live in a civilised nor a well-governed country, and there are hurdles to be jumped. What might be the greatest obstacle, however, which is the matter of the wife in question, is no longer one. She has declared herself willing to be squared. I have been much absent from the house as I have been meeting with her and with divers gentlemen of the long robe . . . She is not against the proposal of a divorce as long as she is compensated for it. All in all she is being a good commonsensical woman about the matter, as I had reason to hope she would. She always was a good and sensible body. There are the expenses to be considered but that will be easily done. I have spoken to Colburn at the magazine and all it will take is some additional work on the terms I've bargained. They are more generous terms than ever I made, Sarah, for I had as excellent a purpose as a man could have in asking them.'

He gripped my hand. 'Sarah, our day is not so far off. All it will take is a little patience, since it cannot be done tomorrow or the next day. But it will be done. And by this same time next year, I swear, you will be Mrs Hazlitt.'

I am sure my hand went dead in his grasp. I had no

notion it had gone so far with him, that he could talk of me cool as a daisy to his wife and to his employer, which is what I had understood him to say.

'I have talked of the matter too with my dear friend Lamb,' he continued. 'He assured me he was very glad to hear of it. He has professed himself happy to receive you if you are inclined to accept the invitation. We may pay him and his sister a visit and dine together with them. Now, what say you, Sarah?'

I saw he considered it a great honour to me that Mr Lamb should agree to receive me. And I dare say it was, Mr Lamb being an eminent author. Mr Roscoe reported that it was said there was to be the most entertaining discourse to be had at his table. And indeed I would be curious to meet Miss Lamb because of her notoriety as a murderess – though I doubt she would display any of her murderous inclinations at table but would be just as ordinary as the rest of us.

However, to go there as the future wife of Mr Hazlitt – well, I had no doubt they would be respectful towards me, whatever their real opinion, if he insisted on it. But since I had not accepted Mr Hazlitt, it would be false in me. Later, when my deception became known, they would despise me for being false and talk of me all over the town.

'I should like to be given forward notice of any engagement to dine at the Lambs,' I told Mr Hazlitt. I was resolved to be ill on the day appointed.

'I promise you shall have good notice,' he said, 'though they are not the kind of people to consider their arrangements much in advance. I am sure your mother could have no objection once she knows it is to the Lambs you are going,' he concluded as if this was my only anxiety.

This was the position in which I now found myself. As good as affianced – ridiculous though it was, the man who was to be my future husband being already in possession of a wife. And I was short to be introduced to his friends, who were, as he had told me, nearer to him than any member of his own family.

To be wife to a man such as no girl dreams of – a man of queer ideas and habits and little sense of everyday life, who walked in the street without a shirt, with his viz ink-stained and hair uncombed, and of an age to be my father – each of his faults of a sudden looked magnified to me.

And all because, I was ready to own, I had allowed myself some experimentation in the practice of kissing and a little more besides, and had agreed to accept some comfort in his arms when it was offered. Because I was alive in the world and wished to taste this fruit and that in it. Because I did not always go into his room with my head bowed down.

But this surely, were he a normal gentleman, should have saved me from his marital ambitions? My little years too – though indeed that seems to only encourage men of an advanced age. After a short while, as I considered my disadvantages – my low place in life, my ignorance, my incapacity to pass in the exalted company he kept – I thought I was foolish to worry. Yet, I was enough anxious not to go near him again for a few days, pleading the headache. When, finding my mornings without him empty, I did go, he was unchanged.

'I feared you were neglecting me,' he protested, 'and giving your morning hours to some other. But the servant told me of your headache and then I resolved to live without you if you would only be well.'

When I would not sit he was more solicitous than cross, and soon resumed his attentions standing up. I attempted a retreat but to a degree was obliged to accept them.

However, he did not refer any more to his divorce. I

began to believe he had perceived my reluctance, or his own error. I believed he was even glad to find me not presuming. Indeed, I began to feel safe. But I was blind, like the big ostrich bird of Africa who buries her head in the sand to avoid the danger that threatens her.

20

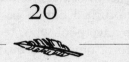

During the month of July in that year I made my first acquaintance with the other gentleman, my dear Henry. At the time, seeing as Mr Hazlitt was absent in Canterbury playing rackets, and, after that, in Crediton, I had not enjoyed a decent conversation with any soul for several days. On account of his absence I was obliged to receive the news of the death of Bonaparte on his rocky island on my own – and was saved in consequence, I am sure, the sight of Mr Hazlitt's grief. But I did mount to his empty room and laid a kiss of condolence, in his place, on the well-loved lips of his little Boney, as I was sure he would have wished.

Returning from a walk, I felt the urgent need of company and turned into Dyer's Buildings to call on my sister. I found the baby downstairs with the nurse and Martha in the parlour stitching a garment for it.

'Your face has gone quite pink,' she exclaimed.

'Well, I am as hot as old scratch,' I said with a laugh.

'A lady should refrain from walking in the heat,' was her reply.

And after that, she was not well disposed to talk, only to complain that she was herself half-suffocated. The air was indeed as dusty and sour as ever it was, but I did not mind it. I am a cold creature who likes to be heated and does not care how it comes. But before we had got too silent and mournful, a visitor was shown in.

This was a young gentleman, at whose arrival my sister forgot all that ailed her and started up with a show of pleasure. She presented him to me as Mr Henry Tompkins. He turned out to be an old chum of Mr Roscoe's from Liverpool who, recently come to London, wished to resume the acquaintance.

From the first I thought him an uncommon pleasing young man. He was good-sized, with nice hay-coloured hair, quiet grey eyes, an excellent complexion, and exceeding clean and neat in his lavish white neckcloth. Mr Tompkins was quite the gentleman. Sober but relaxed in his manner, he was at his ease talking to young ladies and let us know he was pleased by them. He accepted most graceful a cup of lemonade from the jug that Martha kept by her, and soon any touch of starch between us was dispersed. I hoped my complexion was not over-pink, though I was glad of some tint of colour in it, and was flustered to think I was in my second-best gown, and it in so dusty a state too from the streets, and my sash blackened from where it had caught in a carriage axle when I was crossing Holborn. While here was Mr Tompkins, so neat and clean you could think he had been raised clear of the dirt of the streets and was come in his own gig. I feared he might consider me to be slovenly. But I was quick to be careless of the state of my dress as he was so well-mannered.

We talked of the heat in Liverpool, which he assured us was not so great, by comparison at least with London. Next, he brought up the subject of the death of Bonaparte and told us most interesting tales of the rage for mementoes of the old soldier. He himself had seen offered at a great price a slip from the willow that was said to grow over his grave.

'All the same, it cannot but be considered sad,'

suggested Martha, 'that he should end in such a barren place, whatever his faults.'

'I dare say it will look bad for the English in the future, that they put him there,' said Mr Tompkins. 'He was an extraordinary character and a place might have been found for him in the world. But perhaps you could say the same of a tiger or any other dangerous beast.'

In answer to an enquiry from Martha about his purpose for being in London, Mr Tompkins told us he wished to reside here as he was preparing to take his Articles at the Inns. Presently Mr Roscoe came in and the baby was brought up to be admired. Then Mr Tompkins was urged to stay to supper and Martha said I must stay also, so as to make up the table. I fancied he looked pleased when I agreed I would.

I repaired below with my sister to assist her in bringing up the supper. There was a small dish of stewed veal, a very large one of sparrow grass and another of salad, and two sorts of potato. There was a gooseberry tart and an orange jelly, then some cheese – though with none of the disgusting godamitys pigs in it that there so often is at home – and its biscuits and radishes. Martha apologised for the humbleness of the fare and assured Mr Tompkins that if she had known he was to join in it, it would have been a great deal better. He assured her that, on the contrary, it was excellent and ate hearty. As is common with me, I had little appetite.

The gentlemen drank wine. Martha professed herself sorry it was only Portuguese. They talked for a while of politics, Mr Tompkins revealing himself to be not quite the Whig that Mr Roscoe is, and to be an admirer of poor Lord Castlereagh – but not quite a Tory either. Then they fell to speaking of Liverpool and their mutual acquaintances in it and divers personalities my sister and I knew nothing of. I own that once or twice I thought that if Mr Hazlitt were with us the talk might be a great deal more lively. But it could not be so polite.

At the end of it, we all drank port, though you can be sure that Martha and I took only a thimbleful, and Mr Roscoe made the speech he is used to make at table, as he likes nothing better than to pay compliments to his wife.

'Tompkins,' he announced, 'let me heartily recommend to you the married state. Especially if you can arrange to be married to a Miss Walker . . .' Here he smiled at my sister and raised his pot, and I saw Mr Tompkins' gaze pass from her to me. Mr Roscoe, at the same time seeing he had made what might well be considered a blunder, hurried to say he was not intending to be a matchmaker . . . 'But should the present Miss Walker be half as good as her sister she will make an excellent wife.'

I would have liked to protest, as a means of saving face, that to become a wife was not a necessary progression for a Miss Walker, or a girl called by any other name either, but I was too timid, in particular in that company.

When I was leaving them I own I had a little hope that Mr Tompkins might offer to accompany me as far as Southampton Buildings, as old Mr Roscoe had before. The candles were lit, and I could not imagine just then anything nicer than to stroll beside him through the dusk. He was in a deep conversation with Mr Roscoe, however, and though he stood up and gave me his hand it was in an absent manner, and he had taken his seat again before I was gone from the room. In consequence I walked home alone – but, on consideration, I thought such a pleasant evening as I had passed was as much as any girl could hope for.

21

My next opportunity to see Mr Tompkins came about a month later, on Southampton Row. I recognised him at once, in spite of his now wearing a hat, as he had been more than once in my thoughts. I saw him approach – and indeed I hardly know how, as I am hard-pressed to see anything clear – a good head taller than the rest. For modesty's sake I kept my gaze lowered. But I yet had an eye out good enough to observe him hesitate, and come to a stop where I passed him.

'Miss Walker, Miss Walker,' he called out.

I turned and exclaimed with a show of surprise, 'Why, good afternoon, Mr Tompkins.'

'A good afternoon to you,' he replied, and swept off his hat like the born gentleman that he is.

I told him I was going in the direction of the Regent's Park and, after some remarks on the number of passengers wandering in the streets on account of the fine weather, and suchlike pleasantries, he said he had a desire to accompany me as long as I had no objection. I had no objection, of course, and told him so, where-upon he gave me his arm and we strolled along in this graceful style.

It was not my intention that day, I own, to walk in the Park, as you can be quite fagged by going such a distance in the heat. But running into Mr Tompkins, as I had, caused me to fancy the idea. And I hardly wished him to know that I was out on some commonplace errands to do with the house, to fetch a pullet from the Fleet Market and my mother's jug of beer from the Serjeant's and suchlike. A girl likes to show a certain front.

When you are obliged to take a turn out of doors though you may not feel like it, and have no companion, well, at such times the Park, not to speak of the walk there, can seem solitary and melancholy, even with all the fine chariots whirling about. With Mr Tompkins by my side, keeping up a light commentary all the while so I never felt the journey, I thought the Park as gay as ever I saw it. The sheet of water had several pairs of swans in stately motion upon it and the ladies were floating along the paths in their elegant dresses, and the gentlemen no less well turned out, under the darkening foliage – though the place was just as dusty and pungent, I expect, as it was on any day before. After all, I was accompanied by a debonair gentleman of my own. Mr Tompkins told me that he had been making towards the Inns when he observed me coming towards him. And he went to great lengths to reassure me that indeed he was in general diligent, and it was only the sight of a pretty and familiar face such as mine that could divert him from his industry. I was able to accept the compliment with a grateful smile, quite at my ease.

Among the parades of riders and chariots, this one a pea-green curricle, that one near made of glass, I remarked a horse that was more than passing handsome, equipped as he was with crimson housings and fancy stirrups. He passed hard by where we stood, as we admired the view of elegant houses that were gone up. I pointed him out to Mr Tompkins. 'Why, that is the King,' he exclaimed.

The King himself was out taking his exercise, as we were, though he took his on a horse which had to be near as stout as himself to bear him. His outriders were fanned out behind. I felt I must wave to the poor sovereign, though he was already past and could not have seen my excitement.

Mr Tompkins chaffed me in a good-natured way for being such a dutiful subject. 'I am surprised to find you a monarchist, Miss Walker,' he said, 'when the Roscoes are not.'

'I am not devoted to any monarch,' I protested. 'But he is a new king and since he is despised I am sure it would please him to know that not all his subjects hate him. He is a man like any other and would not like a girl who has nothing personal against him to be unfriendly.'

'Well, I am sure it is a nice thing,' he laughed, 'for any man to know.'

In truth I only waved at the King because I was used to do it for any member of his family when I was of an age with Betsy and was lucky enough to see them about. And now I did it without thinking, though not many in London would, such was the happy and generous mood Mr Tompkins put me in.

He would never wish to prevent me from waving at whosoever I wished, he assured me, though he himself would not choose to greet the King. 'Not the king we have just seen, at any rate. Though there may well be another day a sovereign I might be pleased to greet.'

I was glad to know he was not fixed in his views. To be fixed in your views is an arrogant quality and a nuisance to your friends.

As we turned towards home he spoke of his lodgings, which were not satisfactory, being near the Angel and thus inconvenient for the Inns, as well as being cramped for room.

'My mother keeps lodgers,' I informed him, 'and they are convenient; indeed, you could not find any more convenient. Southampton Buildings is but a short step from the Inns. And our lodgers are in general quite contented with us. A proof of it is that we very seldom have an apartment empty.'

He listened to this puff with an air of keen interest, just as he did to everything I had said as we strolled along, while he smiled down upon me, which was necessary, he being so high. I am sure I was more diverting than I am used to on account of it. We sat on a bench to rest and he laid his arm along the rail, without taking any liberties, of course, but in a most considerate way so that I might rest my head upon it.

After that we went much of the way home in silence, but this was not at all hard to bear. Rather, I am sure we were both contemplating how nice an outing it was and were of the one mind and in consequence free from any need to speak.

I left him at the Serjeant's, having told him quite frank of being obliged to fetch the ale. My mother would have well eaten her dinner by now – indeed, it was nearer supper-time – but I thought it best not to go home without it. To bid me goodbye, he took my hand and brushed the tips of my fingers almost fond with his lips.

For some days after this I went out dressed in my walking-trim, as I had a great hope of meeting him again and was confident, when he had seemed so pleased with our acquaintance, that he would be on the look-out for me. But he was nowhere to be seen, and soon I gave up the hope, as a high state of expectation cannot be very long kept up. And I have learned not to be over-expectant when there is a gentleman involved.

At this time, Mr Hazlitt was with us one week and then he could be absent again for two or three. When he was home, I continued in my usual ways, spending my mornings in his room and fetching quantities of his Bohea from Twining's on the Strand near as often as I went out. One day, visiting at my sister's, I overheard Mr Roscoe mention that the young Mr Tompkins was returned to Liverpool. Grieved he was gone so far, and without a word, I made up my mind not to think of him any more. Yet I could not forget him entire. My consolation then was the knowledge that in ten or twenty years, when I was aged, the memory of our walk would return to me as a time that I had once known near-perfect happiness.

22

On account of the withered and lurid leaves the trees in
the gardens looked charred and their trunks ebony-
black, as if the exhalations from all the chimneys, that
were belching again, had scorched them. The sultry
days were passed. I came home from a solitary walk to
find the fire in the parlour lighting and my sister Martha
come to visit. My mother saw fit to entertain her in the
parlour as we saw her but rare now in our house, since
she was Mrs Roscoe, and my mother is sure the parlour
is the only apartment to fit her new station. It was I who
was obliged to pay her the family calls, as my mother has
no taste for walking out or calling. In consequence she
was making a fuss of Martha as if her own daughter
were a more distant relation and one a good deal too
superior to sit in the smoke and steam of the kitchen.
Well, I dare say she is.

Baby Emma was being walked up and down by
Betsy, for she could now totter quite well, and Betsy
was begging to be allowed to take her plaything into the
street so she could show herself off as a nursemaid. At
length she was let and I was sent down to fetch up the
tea-tray. It is a task to which I am accustomed to the
degree that I believe I could do it muffled in a blindfold.

I resolved that we should drink our tea for a change

from the good Nankin china that is taken out even more seldom than my mother sits in the parlour. The sight of the Nankin incited exclamations from my mother when I brought it up and protests from Martha about it being taken out on her account. This was hypocritical of her, since she is content to use her good china in her own house as she pleases.

I was made so cross by their clucking and was so busy pouring, and slicing the plum cake to their liking – thin for my sister's plate, thick for my mother's – and keeping an eye out for Betsy and the baby in the street, that I did not comprehend for some time that they were talking of Mr Tompkins. (This was the same gentleman that I regarded as 'my' Tompkins since the afternoon I had walked out with him.) They were talking of his domestic requirements and his desires in the line of service – from which I learnt, with an upset that dwarfed the first, but was much more happy, that he was to come to live with us.

'My sister is acquainted already with Mr Tompkins,' remarked Martha. 'You do remember him, Sarah, do you not?'

I put on as a defence against her enquiry a vacant expression, though indeed I had little reason to.

'You met in my house some months ago,' she persisted.

'Sally lets on to forget things she has every knowledge of,' sighed my mother. 'She has not forgotten him, I am sure, if he is as fine a young gentleman as you say.' She winked an eye at Martha. 'In any case, I am sure she will remember him soon enough.'

'He was very keen to take the room,' agreed Martha, with something of the same winking smirk, 'and his keenness increased, I believe, once I mentioned Sarah. But then, he is going on for the law and must cultivate a long memory.'

'Not like Sal, who has nothing to think about except chaynie cups and her new shawl,' my mother said in her mock-sighing way. Now that she was seated over tea in the parlour she liked to pretend that I have nothing to do all day and she was keeping her daughter fresh and dainty and leisured as the young lady of the house.

She and my sister resembled two matchmakers plotting in a corner, though I cannot say that displeased me just then to any great degree.

'He is not to have anything out of my room,' I said with a show of crossness, to dispel any notions they might have about my liking Mr Tompkins.

'There is nothing in it for him to have, I'm sure, since Mr Hazlitt got the satinwood,' my mother said. 'Though I don't believe Mr Hazlitt has any appreciation of it. It is my opinion he is not quite the gentleman your father thinks him. He would be just as contented with the old oaken chest. But we cannot do an exchange. Mr Hazlitt is the kind of man to remark it when he never did before, and decide to take offence.'

To this I agreed. And then Betsy came in, as my niece would not lie down for her and sleep like a doll as she wished she would. And my sister finished her tea and took her leave.

Until Mr Tompkins came a week later there was no talk but of his room – which was to be the one old Mr Bulrose was gone from off the first landing – and the arrangement of it. Although indeed it was only talk and little enough done – except on my part. I went up with my wax and dusting-cloths and brushes and laden with complements of linen and a bushel of candles. My mother never went near it only to put her head in once – and then she found me seated on the bed in a reverie. Whereupon she told me to put a hurry on – though she did remark, quite proud, as if it were all her own work, that it looked finer than it was used to. And she wished she could have it for herself and only might, she supposed, when she was on her deathbed. And she agreed I was not a bad-working girl when I put my mind to something. She made no objection to Mr Tompkins' having the good brocade counterpane that I had spread on his bed, nor the silver-plated candlestick I polished to a shine.

After admitting the new lodger, and a fellow to carry his boxes, she declared him to be an uncommon fine-looking man. 'He is of an excellent size and well turned-out,' she said at the supper-table. 'I hope Sally will do for him with the same care she does for Mr Hazlitt, as I am sure he merits it as much.'

'I am sure Mr Tompkins may be a well-looking fellow,' my father put in, 'but Mr Hazlitt is a great one.'

This put a stop to the discussion and we heard no more for that evening concerning the qualities, good or bad, of the lodgers.

I found myself quite agitated outside Mr Tompkins' room with his tray in the morning. He had asked to be summoned early to breakfast, so that he might be at his place at the Inns in good time. He was still abed in his chamber as I set out his coffee, which is what he took, being a true Englishman and a gentleman, of a morning. He came to the table still dazed and greeted me with no more than a sleepy, 'Ah, it is Sarah indeed.'

But by and by as he ate his muffin he came to himself, and was easy and cheerful and told me I was an excellent girl for making coffee. I laughed and remarked I was said to be excellent for many things — surprising myself, as I did not mean to be immodest. But he showed no displeasure and laughed also. 'I am sure you are,' he said, 'and I intend to find them out.'

His neck was bare, as he was not yet dressed, and it was still soft and rosy from his sleep and very agreeable to glimpse when he lowered his cup and made light conversation. He said that Southampton Buildings was indeed most convenient to the Inns and, besides that, he was well contented, since he was acquainted with our family and had such good reports of the house.

I replied that we felt it an honour to have him, and other commonplace courtesies, and that we were all, my mother and my brother and myself, and my little sister too, at his disposal for whatever services he might require; he had only to ask, though they were out of the ordinary run itself, he was not to hesitate. He mentioned he would like his boots blacking and I said Betsy would do it. Which she does with pleasure, for she is glad of the penny.

I withdrew then to leave him to dress. He did not make a reference to our unexpected outing that we took together in the summer. But something in his manner reassured me that he remembered it and that it was only a measure of his respect for me that he did not refer to it.

'What a nice contented girl you look this morning,' remarked my mother as I sat over my own coffee and muffin in the kitchen. And indeed I had been contemplating that the place had an uncommon pleasing aspect with a soft light filtering in through the window though it was clouded with the grime from the street. And Lizzie's humming as she slopped out her basins was not so tiresome as it could be. Mother pinched my cheek and remarked my colour was improving and bade me then to make haste with Mr Hazlitt's service. She could not have his high opinion of the house disappointed.

'I shall come down direct and wash that window,' I announced, 'for it is very dirty.'

'You may wash where you wish, I'm sure,' she said in surprise. 'But there is a deal more upstairs waiting on a wash than the kitchen window what nobody sees but ourselves.'

Our own comforts, apart from the comforts of the table, are not something my mother thinks a great deal of, as we are not paid for them.

23

I do not say I neglected Mr Hazlitt once Mr Tompkins was come. But I do own I could have, had Mr Hazlitt allowed me to neglect him. If I were delayed of a morning for even five minutes on account of the extra work Mr Tompkins occasioned, for I liked to do everything nice for him, I was like to find Mr Hazlitt waiting at his door for me with a greater eagerness than my niece waited on her sugared mush. Why, you could fancy you heard him make little eager whimpers as she did.

But it was not his breakfast toast he was waiting on. Before he would consent to touch it he would have to stroke my hand or my hair, as if he sought to reassure himself I lived. And he would beg for an embrace – though I did not always grant it, as I was determined not to be as free with him in the future as I was in the past. When he stared at me with that sombre and watchful gaze he has – and it was there even when I turned my back to him, for I knew it to bore into me as much as the wood might know the nail – I felt his whole being bent hungry upon me, as if he wished from me every ounce of sustenance and nourishment that any being might ever hope to squeeze from another. And at that it would not be enough. I could not see any way of giving him more than a little portion of what he wanted.

But how was I to tell him so? If I knew how, and had courage enough to attempt it, he would assault me with whys and wherefores and demands for details that I had no capacity to provide. And after long speeches from him and flushed stumbled words from me, we would arrive back at the spot towards which he always directed me, the spot he would not move an inch from.

'Tell me, Sarah. You are fond of me? Even a little?' I murmured a reluctant 'yes'.

'This is joy . . . This is paradise itself to me, to hear you assent to even a little fondness for me now and then . . . Oh Sarah, I cannot, I will not, live in the absence of that little affection you hold for me. You are all in the world to me, Sarah. And I intend, and you know it too, to do all that is necessary so I might be your all too before very long.'

Here he would look at me with a great and soulful significance. At my silence, for I had no need to enquire what it was that was necessary, he would seek to reassure himself. 'Do you hang your head, Sarah? Do you show so little joy at the prospect? But of course you do. For you are a good girl who does not feel free to speak her heart in the unfree circumstances such as ours are.'

Or he might grow playful and remark, 'A practical maid like my Sally does not like to count her chickens till they are hatched. Eh, Sally?' And like this he would be cheerful and draw me to him again, as if we might resume our game. But he was too serious and too intent behind it all to let me feign to myself any more that it was a game like I might have preferred.

It was no bad thing for all concerned that Mr Hazlitt and Mr Tompkins took little notice of each other. Mr

Tompkins was not unconscious of Mr Hazlitt's eminence in the literary world, but he is not himself a literary man, being too much occupied with his studies at the Inns, and took no more than a minor interest in him.

As to his fellow-lodger's other qualities, he saw in him only an elderly man who kept irregular hours, so that they seldom so much as passed on the stairs. And indeed Mr Hazlitt, as he might be spied in the house or in the street, wrapped up in his brooding thoughts, showed little of the intensity and vigour he displayed in his own chambers – and then only in the company of a person who was well acquainted with him, as I was. As for Mr Tompkins, I don't believe Mr Hazlitt for a long time ever took any notice of him.

He took little notice of anyone in the house outside of me. He hardly noticed Cajah, though Cajah was always skulking on the stairs observing him, or tailing him in the street as a diversion, or keeping an eye on his antics at the Fives. That is Cajah for you, let play the young master since he likes the part, and my mother is pleased to encourage him in it.

I would see Mr Tompkins and Mr Hazlitt pass on the stairs and Mr Tomkins raise his hat. And Mr Hazlitt, lacking a hat and so unable to return the courtesy, continue down without any acknowledgement of this good-looking young man, and he residing in what you could say was his own house. But I dare say it was because he was pondering on me or the essay he was writing, so a stray fellow like Mr Tompkins could mean little to him.

If I found myself on the stairs when they were both on it I took care to put on a show of hurry, for fear that one of them might display to the other the nature of his friendship with me. I did not wish Mr Hazlitt to come to a stop, and his expression to change and his voice to turn soft and glad, and Mr Tompkins to mark it. And I was in no doubt it would put Mr Hazlitt into an unreasonable gloom to hear Mr Tompkins chaff me and invite me to his room or out for a stroll – though I wished dear that he would indeed.

In consequence I would hasten past, and let them wonder at it if they wished. A girl in my situation has to look to her own safeguard, even though she may find it disagreeable and not quite honest. Honesty is a luxury only the ladies can afford. I wished Mr Hazlitt to think well of me. But his power over me was waning the more he declared his devotion. For Mr Tompkins now I had the more tender and ready feeling. The blood flew hot into my face when I fancied I heard his step on the stair in the evening. When his door slammed as he left us in the morning I was cast down and the prospect of the whole day ahead when he would be gone seemed like a dry sahara. On occasion he might come back early, at two or three o'clock, with a paper of chops under his arm. And I do believe no thirsty nomad ever saw the oasis with such delight as I saw him, though it might be only to pass him with my pail and besom. And then I would be cross and shamed as well that he had caught me in the character of the damp and soiled maid-of-all-work.

In the morning when I went to wait on him, I worried that I did not look well or my gown was dirty. I would be breathless fit to faint wondering how he would greet me and how I might conduct myself. But my feet, surer than I, would fly before me at the prospect and, finding myself in his room, all my worries were melted away by his easy manner. I would steal glimpses of him while he applied the razor to his fair silky stubble, and plunged his face in the basin, and arranged his neckcloth before the glass with a frown that made me love him all the more, it was so rare. I knew he respected me and I was able to regard myself with the same esteem with which I viewed him.

I soon learned that he had four sisters at home who waited on him like I did, as they had but one servant, who was old and crippled and indeed herself needed waiting on. His sisters kept the kitchen too, it was a country house where they did not believe in show and ceremony. He gave no impression that he saw me as a piece of tasty game to be hunted like so many gentlemen do, and I was contented to play the part of a tender sister to her good brother for a change. After such an exchange he would mark the time and run off to the Inns. He was, despite his easy ways, a serious fellow, conscious of his sisters' hopes and the charge he was to his family.

When the morning was well advanced I would go up to Mr Hazlitt, near-fearful and near as burdened in my mind as my hands were with his breakfast-tray, for he was presuming, and pushing me to a degree I had little reason to welcome. I did not wish him to put aside one wife with no assurance of having another, which was his only purpose, as far as I could see, in going to all the trouble and expense of a divorce. But I could find no means of telling him so. He was so fixed in his own opinions and had not the slightest intention of taking in a fact he had no desire to. I do not say he was dull or caused me to be dull. Indeed it was the opposite, because his great brain could not be still. He had so many things in his head to occupy him from morning till night – which is why I fancy he rose so late or he would have dropped down in the afternoon from the clamour in it.

I was much-worked after Mr Tompkins came to live with us, having a new gentleman to wait on, and out of weariness my attention was apt to wander when Mr Hazlitt spoke. He seldom remarked it, for his flight of words was a pleasure to him. 'There is no one I can talk with as I can with you,' he would declare. 'Apart from dear Lamb, to a degree. But that is different. A girl, when he truly loves her, can inspire a man to thoughts and sentiments and their connections in a way which other men have spoken of, but that I never knew till now. Love is a flame that ignites genius in a man. Mine never took light before, wanting the right girl. But now they shall see what I can do . . . And you will continue to be my tinder-box, won't you Sarah? For a little while at least?'

He did not like monotony, for he was always coming and going. He went often to Winterslow, a place I fancied I knew well, for I addressed his letters there and he was never done speaking of it as his ideal country. In the month of December he was there, and was hardly back a week before he went off again into Berkshire to report on a boxing match.

I believe these respites I had, from him and the press of his sentiments, saved me from suffocation, as well as him from the truth. Granting me the opportunity to miss his company, when I had no one else in the house to offer any, I would appreciate it afresh. And they allowed me to believe I could be in no great danger from him, seeing as he could go off and leave me with such regularity.

In that week he was with us he arrived home one afternoon proud and smiling, holding a boy's hand fast in his. He made sure to catch me on the stairs. 'Sarah,' he said, with a great show of ceremony, 'I wish you to meet my son, William.' And he thrust the boy forward to shake my hand, as I held out my own.

But the child refused me. 'I do not like to shake hands with girls,' he said with a frown.

I did but laugh, for it is not uncommon in a boy to take that attitude. I offered to take up some tea to them and, when the offer was accepted, went out to the confectioner's to fetch some iced buns such as boys like. When I went up with the tray, Mr Hazlitt was inspecting his son most fond as the boy read out a passage of his, and did not seem to mind that he smudged it with his finger.

Later, when I was in the passage, I ran into William as he came back from the small-house. He stopped and looked at me appraising in a way I did not like.

'I do not find you pretty,' he announced. 'Whatever my father may say, I think he is mistaken. You are scrawny and poor-looking indeed.'

Again I laughed, but in a more forced manner than I had before. And I kept out of the way of either of the Hazlitts until they quit the house. I thought the younger was sure to grow up to have his father's worst characteristics of pride and arrogance but none of his better tender ones.

24

There was a hard frost the day that Mr Hazlitt set off for Berkshire to see the fight. The smoke, lifting here and there, displayed a frugal but enlivening glow from the sun and a sky raising itself out of its general drear to the pale Nankin blue of our good tea-set. I believe there never was such a well-looking day – though there was another reason also for me to think so. Every conveyance in the streets, from the humblest wagon to the nimblest fly, was clad in white hoar, when they are otherwise clogged with divers hues of grey. They wore the icy glitter you could dream up for a princess's coach in a fairy-tale. The clouds of smoke floating about in the tasty air came as much from the drifting breaths of the swathed passengers as from the countless hearths puffing their exhalations up the chimneys.

In the early afternoon I went out for a few articles. As I was turning the corner of Fleet Street I ran straight into Mr Tompkins. He was just coming out after taking his dinner at the Bell.

'If you will agree to be detained,' he said with a gay smile, 'let us take advantage of this refreshing air. Would you care to stroll along with me in the direction of the Thames? I should like to see if it is frozen over.' He was eager to step out on the ice and skate as he had heard the Cockneys to do, and I hoped dear for his sake it would be frozen.

Placing my hand in the nook of his arm he found it chilled, in spite of my wearing my mittens. He tucked it in tight, and commenced to chafe the fingers of my hand that was still at liberty, to warm them. As we went along, he showed himself very curious and interested in all kinds of things concerning me. What had I for occupation when the gentlemen had gone off in the morning to their divers employs? Was my favourite activity reading? Or was it mending or embroidering? And so on.

I gave as good an account of myself as I could. That I preferred to work flowers than patches as they were more artistic. That I liked indeed to read – though I did not say the only books I had the time to attempt of late were Mr Hazlitt's.

'And the play, do you like to go to see the play?' he asked.

'I cannot say,' I replied, 'for I am not in the habit of going.'

He told me he did not greatly care for it himself but he believed the ladies in general did. His sisters considered the play must be the best of diversions. Should I like to go sometime, he asked, to Covent Garden or Drury Lane? He was too occupied at present and, besides, could not see his way to bearing the expense, but he would like to know what the theatre in London was and its actors that were spoken so high of.

I took his remarks as an invitation and was most flattered, you can be sure. 'We might make up a company with the Roscoes,' I ventured.

This, I feared, was forward of me as he did not assent, though he did not refuse the suggestion either.

Arriving at the Thames, we found it not frozen over after all, though it had a glassy look, and thin wafers of ice where the viscous-looking water lapped on the shale.

'I fear there will be no skating to be had on the river this time,' declared Mr Tompkins.

He had so sorrowful a tone, but so comical too in his tragedy — like a child baulked of a much-desired plaything — that I could not hold back from laughing. And he laughed too, though he made a good show of being offended, and assured me that he would fling me into the river as an experiment, since I was a light little body who looked as if she might skate on a wafer, if I were not solemn that instant. But I could not stop from laughing, even had I wanted to, and when I kept on he plucked me from my standing as easy as Betsy takes her doll and swung me out over the iron sheet of water. And it was such a thrill as he held me so tight, and I had no fear of being dropped. Indeed when he put me down safe again, I was sorry.

We were of a mind for sport of any kind. However, there was little good to be had in stopping there to watch the passing scene as it was too cold to sit, and the passengers, wrapped up alike in shawls and greatcoats, were as hooped and dull as a motley flock of monks, all bent on hurrying along towards some cheerful fireside. I could not have cared if I never saw a fire again. I was quite warm enough strolling along with Mr Tompkins, his gloved hand clasping mine to keep it from icing up.

Without any discussion of the matter, we turned as one towards Waterloo Bridge, which, being so new, is said to make the finest promenade in London and, as you must pay a penny to walk on it, is free of the inconveniences of the thronged thoroughfares. Mr Tompkins paid the toll and its space and elegance were ours, its views spread out before us to observe in ease and comfort. To the right and left were Westminster and Blackfriars, covered with the never-ending crowd, black and, in the distance, like lines of writing on a page. I could not make out all that Mr Tompkins exclaimed at, the spires and towers and patches of fields, golden in the sunlight. But I saw the handsome river front of Somerset House hard by, and the great ball of Saint Paul's, and I believe I could make out the towers of Westminster Abbey rising up. Beneath us there were the ships and coal-barges beating along, and seeming to labour in the thickening water. I lay in against Mr Tompkins as we gazed east and west, and up and down. His coat was stiffening from the icy coagulates.

'Sarah's hand is unfortunately more pervious to ice than the river,' he remarked, squeezing it tender, 'being a small and fragile thing.'

As we were wending our way homeward along the Strand, with the same reluctance, I'm sure, on both sides, he drew up outside the Crown and Anchor. 'We might step in here,' he suggested, 'and take a hot punch to warm us.'

The Crown and Anchor is not a low place, by any means. But still I hesitated, though I was keen to go in. I feared he might think ill of me if I did. But, reckless or no, in a moment I found myself inside, and was led on his arm up to the great blazing fire, and seated next to it. Inside a minute I was so warmed I was obliged to remove my shawl and mittens. A sherry negus was brought to me. I found I liked it well, though I am not in the habit of taking such refreshment. Soon any doubts I had remaining melted away, as the Crown and Anchor is quite a respectable inn with a fine high ceiling. It was dark and smoky from the fires and the tobacco-pipes, but the candles were already lighting. There was little notice taken of me except by the serving-man.

'That is a fine little lass you have brought in to visit us,' he remarked to Mr Tompkins.

This was a nice courtesy. Since the man was acquainted with Mr Tompkins, the Crown and Anchor being a haunt of his, he wished to pay him a compliment. My modest manner and appearance commanded respect, I'm sure, which indeed I can not say of some of the other ladies present. I accepted another negus, well sugared and spiced, when it was offered and our health was drunk with a clatter of pots. I was more than contented seated there by the fire listening to Mr Tompkins' talk with his companions. I remember they spoke of the mail-coaches and the rate of speed of the Portsmouth mail in comparison to the mail on the Liverpool road, which Mr Tompkins professed himself not too pleased with. His sisters, I dare say, complained that his letters were delayed, as they would be waiting impatient on them, you can be sure, just as I would be were I in the way of receiving messages from him. And they spoke of the expense of transport of any kind, whether for letters or passengers, unless you were happy to have your bones shaken about on a journeyman's cart.

'It is a great obstacle to progress,' said Mr Tompkins, 'and makes for a backward population when a man cannot get about.'

I wondered whether I should speak up and let them know Mr Roscoe's opinion on the subject, which is that we are in a time of great alteration and forward motion – and though it is hard to imagine what change the future will bring, the diversity of machines will be its engine. If we have steamships, he says, we may have steam-coaches too. I knew it was Mr Hazlitt's belief, however, that we are in retrograde motion, that we have lived in a time when liberty and progress held out their hands to us and we did not grasp them. I decided to remain silent, as I did not wish to err on either side and have an acquaintance of Mr Tompkins laugh at my stupidity.

To sit in such a place as the Crown and Anchor struck me as an excellent way to while away the day if you were a gentleman, with friends, and strangers too, if you tired of them, of every class and shape to entertain you. I did not wonder any more at Mr Hazlitt's liking for the taverns. Indeed, I marvelled that he sought to spend his time with me instead of in a place such as this where his morosity could be lightened and his speech better appreciated.

A gentleman acquaintance of Mr Tompkins wished to offer me yet another glass. But I turned him down. I own I might have been happy enough to take it if I had not remarked that Mr Tompkins was not persuaded I should. That is but one way a girl can be ruined. There are hazards that may lead to ruin on every side. Maybe I might as well have gone that road as the way Mr Hazlitt sent me. It would be my own doing and I might be merry as I did.

When we were in the street again, I asked Mr Tompkins whether he considered it light in a girl to go into a tavern.

'When she is with a friend,' he said, 'she may go where she pleases.' And he gave me a squeeze.

I asked him whether his sisters were happy to enter a tavern. He replied with a laugh that he hoped they would not. Then, quick as a flash, he changed his opinion and said that he had no doubt they would if they had the chance, but this was not likely given their place in life.

Flurries of snow began to come down and whirl about us. Mr Tompkins took an arm from the sleeve of his coat and settled it for shelter around my shoulders. Like that we were of necessity pressed close together as we walked along. It was dusk as we went up Chancery-lane, jolly as grigs. With the swirling of the snow you could not make out a face though it loomed right up in front of yours.

As we were passing Chichester Rents I felt him press upon my shoulder to divert our route. Once we were some way up the alley and well out of sight of the passengers on the thoroughfare – though they could not have made out a thing in any case, it was so fuzzy – he steered me into a doorway that was little used and caught me compulsive to him and fair bruised my mouth with the press of his own. It was a paining kiss but sweet. He near lifted me off my feet with his fervour.

I was surprised he did not attempt any more than a kiss. If he had, I am not sure I would have been capable of offering any great resistance, such was the tenderness of my feelings for him. But he was a boy in comparison with Mr Hazlitt, and was never married, and hardly, I'm sure, a regular user of the women of the town. Well, he would not have the ready tin in the first place to compensate them.

At the entrance to Lincoln's Inns, he left me, but with a great deal of reluctance. He said he was late but that it meant nothing to him, as a man could not be always huddled over his books but had to have a little diversion on occasion. I could see the degree to which he was taken with me and went home near dizzy at the thought that what I had long hoped for had come about. I knew myself to be mistress of his heart – for that short while, at any rate.

25

I was the possessor of his heart, Mr Hazlitt informed me every day we were together. But I did not want it. This is the sadness of the games the heart plays, that its object is so rarely obedient. It is like the ball in the hands of a bad player at rackets, flying about the hall like a bird let out of its cage. The heart may be happy to be caged, but seldom by the one that seeks to catch it.

When Mr Hazlitt came back from the country he kept to his room for some days, at first sleeping off the journey, and then writing his essay about the fight that he had gone to see.

He read passages out to me as he went along. His style was so vivid that I near believed I was there at his side as he tramped the frosty road in the dawn on his way to find out the field where the boxers were to meet, and that I too stood and cheered as the Gasman's blow followed the Bull's and vice versa, one after the other. Though I'm sure it's a bad thing for a man to box his fellow and nearly as bad to watch and cheer him on. Why, you can see a fight any day of the week you like in London, you only have to go as far as Whitechapel.

But Mr Hazlitt made it all so plain and good-natured that you could regard the Bull's fight with the Gasman as an engagement of champions, as though it were a

battle between two noble knights of old England –
though I believe no one ever made them so lively – and
you quite forgot your prejudice against the business. I
was surprised that he put himself so much in it. He
wrote how he went hither and thither in search of the
coach, and the kind of inn he put up at, and what he ate
for his supper and what the gentlemen talked of. I
marvelled that he brought it so much to life.

If I were not so fearful of the pen, I would like to
write in the same way. My writing could not have the
interest of a fight to recommend it, but I would like to
show how a girl such as I am lives, how she thinks and
feels and how she passes her days – in place of putting
forward only what a girl ought to be – that is, white as
French milk that has the cream skimmed off – which is
what all the writers do. Mr Hazlitt, for all he could
compose so vivid and with such an appearance of the
truth, told only lies when he came to write about me.

Just then Christmas was coming up. As a seasonal
token of his affection, I dare say, he issued to me an
invitation to accompany him to see the play at Covent
Garden. 'We shall have a box, Sarah,' he said, as a means
of coaxing me. 'Since I am a critic I am given a box.
And I shall order up a cabriolet to carry us there, for I
would not like you to catch cold.'

The play he selected for us to see was *Romeo and
Juliet*. He had often talked of its greatness. Maybe he
hoped to incite in me some of the extremes of feeling of
Juliet, so I could be a more fitting object for his Romeo.
Also he thought as much of the actor Macready who
was playing in it as he did of his prize-fighters.

I had hoped he might invite the Roscoes to join us,
for then we would have a proper party and I might be
better amused by confiding my observances to my sister
in a manner I would not to him, as he would be sure to
think me trivial. In place of them, he invited my

mother, who indeed had no great desire to accept, as she takes little pleasure in fine words. He might well have pleased her better by taking her along to see the Gas and the Bull boxing in a field. However, it was cunning of him to ask her, as he could well hope she would doze off by and by, and my attention be devoted to him when she did. She agreed to accept, as much out of a wish to please my father by favouring this important lodger of his as out of any wish to please Sal, I'm sure.

It was fortunate that Mr Tompkins was absent in Liverpool for the holiday. In consequence there was no necessity for him to know anything about my going off to Covent Garden without him. I feared he could be pained, since he had been the first to bring up the idea. As to dress, I was promised a new gown for Christmas. And now it was quickly made up to be ready for the play. This is my green and buff. At that time it was in the newest style, with full sleeves and skirt and a wadded hem. The seamstress wondered whether for full perfection I might consider the wearing of stays. Not in an attempt to decrease the stomach, as so many ladies must, but to swell the embonpoint, which in my case is but a modest feature.

'Mercy,' my mother exclaimed, 'she is fine enough as she is.' But I believe she would have let me have them, only my sister was quick to let her know that she considered stays too brazen and forward for a girl of my looks and station. That is all very well for her to say, since, where I have two little cockagees under my bodice for bubs, she has a pair of plump Worcester pearmains. However, she was good enough to lend me her best shawl, which was green with a patterned edge and a good match for my gown.

I would have liked to have a pair of the pantalettes that are finished with a flounce, such as you see on some modish young ladies when they are strolling in the Park.

But my mother would not lay out the expense for that kind of show. I was to be considered fortunate to be given drawers. They made Lizzie squeal, though she was impressed too, that I was quite the lady in them. My mother would wear nothing but her best. This is a gown as aged as it is old-fashioned, a plain high-waisted thing which hangs limp about her like a chemise. She would hear of no improvement and declared that a wife of her age and station might surely enjoy the comfort at last of not being troubled about her dress.

When the day for the play came round I was excused from doing my usual work after dinner so as to be well rested. I passed the afternoon at a most thorough toilet, at which Betsy assisted me. She spent a long time curling and pinning up my hair and declared I was as good as Polly to dress, as I sat as motionless. My mother, though she refused any assistance, since she was sure she could not be made better than she was, made ready in good time. We were seated by six in the parlour to await our escort, my mother grumbling all the while that indeed she was sure she would much rather stay at home.

At last Mr Hazlitt came down – and I declare I hardly knew him he looked so elegant. I believe the snow-white shirt was his own and bought new. But he must have borrowed his coat from some gentleman-friend, for I never saw it before or after in his room. I thought none the worse of him for that but took it as a compliment. Was I not wearing my sister's shawl, which I had borrowed? On my bosom lay the golden heart with the lock of his hair in it that I had put on half to please him, though also I found it looked very well with my gown. I saw his eyes rest on it with a hidden look of pleasure and was myself pleased that it had the intended effect.

'I do not believe there will be a more elegant pair of

ladies to be seen in the theatre tonight,' he exclaimed, smiling upon us.

It was gracious of him to say so indeed, since my mother appeared quite dowdy.

'We can return the compliment, I'm sure,' she responded.

He took her hand in his and raised it to his lips to show he was touched by her graceful speech – though, as he did, he gazed significant at me over her head. He left us then to go out to Oxford Street to hunt up our cabriolet.

I had not yet sat in a cabriolet – and had been much longing to, since they were only come recent on the streets. To step up as if it were your own carriage, and your own coachman at your bidding to drive you wherever you please, it is a most elegant way to travel – well, as long as you have the money to pay on your arrival. Mr Hazlitt is not shabby in that way and could make a display of riches when he wished.

The knocker was struck, and quick we gathered our shawls and ridicules and went down. And there was the cabriolet, looming up in front of us in its smart coffee-brown paint and our driver in attendance. The steps were let down and Mr Hazlitt first assisted my mother up, though with no small difficulty on account of the stiffness in her back. When it was my turn I was careful to step up modest and elegant, as I observe ladies to do when they mount into a landau. I am sure I showed not an inch of my stockings to view.

Seated between my mother and Mr Hazlitt as we set off, I was drawn but once to reflect that it was something of a pity it was not Mr Tompkins at my side. The ideal, I dare say, is not to be had in life. But I was at that time still fond of Mr Hazlitt – and might be yet were he not so unreasonable in his conduct. For I am not a girl who likes to be affrighted by a man. I like him to be quiet and ordered in his moods, though he might let himself go a little wild in his kisses, sure enough. Just then Mr Hazlitt was so gracious and collected in himself and so elegant dressed – and scented too, I am sure, for the cab was filled with a delicious smell of flower water that was not mine nor Mother's either – that I was more than contented with him. I was also contented with myself, for I was nice attired, and that is always part of a girl's happiness.

He and my mother made commonplace talk about the multitudes in the streets and the uproar the town was in, it coming up to Christmas. Meantime, without her remarking the movement, he took my hand and placed it stealthy inside his shirt, where I found, reposing on his naked chest, the gold heart that had a coil of my hair in it. It lay just above his own invisible beating one. 'You see? We are of the one heart,' he murmured in my ear. Whereupon, after a squeeze, he returned the hand to my lap again and buttoned up his shirt front, all the while responding with warm attention to my mother's remarks on the divers folk in the streets as we passed them by at a smart trot.

Coming up to the theatre, we were obliged to slow to a near-halt as we joined the jam of conveyances that were lining up in the order of their arrival in front of the entrance. There was hardly one among them that was not in good trim. When it came to our turn to alight, Mr Hazlitt jumped out first and handed us down one by one with a flourish.

I had never before been out in public with him, we were always in his room. Strange it was to see him in the light of an escort, amid a scene so impressing. I did not know how to take him. But when mother took his left arm, I knew I might take the other. He had told me he would take a box for us, but I was resolved not to expect it, as I was sure he was as liable as men in general are to make extravagant promises and I would not like to be disappointed. But once inside, we had only a moment to look about us at the place hung with scarlet and gold before we were taken by a liveried lackey and were led up the grand stairs to the boxes. He could not have shown us any greater sign of respect by his manner than if we had possession of the box every week of the year or had come from the court itself to see the play. I am sure anyone who remarked our sedate passage as we followed him could think so.

I own I had not full understood the importance of a box. Once we were settled in ours, I saw the necessity of it. There is nothing like a box for the privacy it affords, and to be seen at your best and to yourself see the play to its best advantage. I confess I would not have been half so happy to be down among the mob, even if it meant I might have better made out the actors. As Mr Hazlitt writes on the strengths and weaknesses of the play for the magazines, he must needs have an excellent vantage. As for me I saw it, I fear, as a scene shrouded in fog, this on account of my weak eyesight.

But to see real figures moving about below and crying out their speeches – that they were far off and lacked detail made it, I am sure, all the more tragic and romantic. A lady in the box next to us peered at the scene through a pair of glasses and must have made it out well in consequence. But she was elderly and I would not like to look ugly and to draw attention to myself by using such a contrivance.

By and by I knew from my mother's little grunts and starts, the same that she produces when she dozes by the fire, that she was no longer attending. Mr Hazlitt too soon knew it, for his arm stole about my shoulder and next his hand took mine that was lying in my lap. And in place of watching the figures far below on the stage, he bent his gaze upon my profile.

I dare say that to make a close inspection of my reactions was a source of enjoyment for him, seeing as he was often at the play and accustomed to the novelty of it. However, considering it not discreet of him to make such an open display of his affection, I obliged him after a little while to remove his arm from my shoulder. I did allow him in recompense to leave where it was the hand that clasped mine, as that could be marked by no one. I was glad I did. For when Romeo cried out, 'See how she leans her cheek upon her hand – Oh that I were a glove upon that hand, that I might touch that cheek', Mr Hazlitt was at liberty to press my hand, thus letting me know that he too felt the same force of sentiment.

The curtain dropped to signify the interval. At this Mr Hazlitt stood and said we might now stroll about. My mother could not be got to stir and sent us off arm in arm to take our place in the throng. What most seized my interest, amidst all the glitter of spangles and finery, though I lowered my head at the sight, was the array of painted beldams, who, though they are wretched souls and wear their black satins and carmine cheeks as a costume to announce it, looked quite pretty – a few among them, at any rate. And there were some who I remarked to smile friendly at Mr Hazlitt – but then, they are the sort to smile at any gentleman, whether they are acquainted with him or no. I could not but pity them, for a girl may be pretty as a picture, but her looks are of no account if she has lost her character. Then she is only an ill-fated creature on whom all eyes, even the tenderest, look with scorn.

When we took our places in the box again, Mr Hazlitt's arm travelled once more around my shoulders. This time I did not shake it off but left it there. When Romeo declared, 'Oh, I am fortune's fool', Mr Hazlitt rested his head upon mine for a moment to show he did not share the inquietude. 'That, my sweet Sarah,' he whispered, 'is what I shall never have to say to you.'

Then Juliet and her Romeo were lying dead on the ground. And I am obliged now to think it was for the best. With such enemies as they had, they were never to find happiness in this world.

In the midst of the multitude, who were all gay and chattering as if they had been present at a comedy, we made our way down the stairs. I hardly marked their finery, seeing them through the same fog that I had seen the play – but now it was because my eyes were full with tears. Though I made sure not to shed them, as to weep would mar my looks. My mother, who had woken up at the end as prompt as if a bell was rung, was yawning heartily while protesting every minute that she had never seen a wonder to match what we had just seen.

'I am glad you think so, Mrs Walker,' Mr Hazlitt was saying, making a gracious pretence at believing her as he made way for us through the mill.

Outside, our cab was waiting on us, and not far behind in the line either, having come on Mr Hazlitt's instructions to fetch us home. It was only when we were seated in it, and going with a stop and a start down Bow Street on account of the crush of carriages, that he turned to me.

'And you, Sarah, tell me, did the play please you?'

'You saw how it pleased me,' I answered.

'I did. But I should like to hear you say it,' he said, and I thought he was not curious how I should reply but only wished to hear me speak.

''Tis not a particular story,' I ventured.

'And how so?'

''Tis a tragedy,' I said, 'that could happen just as well in London as in Verona. Love, all the more when it is true, can be crossed and hindered anywhere in the world. There are always those who will get in the way of lovers and hinder them.' Here I was thinking of Mr Bradley. He was not a Ghibelline and I was by no means a Guelph, but his family's opposition came between us just as much as if we were.

'Well, Sarah, I cannot think what you, at your age, can know of love,' protested my mother. And she poked me in my side, under cover of the darkness inside the cab, for she did not consider it wise in a girl to talk so knowing in front of a gentleman. But I was used to plain speaking with Mr Hazlitt.

'Why so?' he persisted. 'You consider true love to be always hopeless?'

'Yes,' I said. 'They do not like it. They prefer a love that is founded only on good sense.'

'Quite right too,' exclaimed my mother. 'I am sure Mr Hazlitt can see no harm in that. Nor, I am sure, sir, can Sarah.' And she leaned over to Mr Hazlitt and patted him on the knee to persuade him of the truth of what she had said. Then she sat back in a huff.

'I am not one of them,' whispered Mr Hazlitt in my ear. 'Though I fear true love sometimes appears to make little sense when its object is a certain Miss Walker.'

This was a light speech and could be taken several ways, so I was able to return his smile.

He could be agreeable when he wished. But he had other qualities not so agreeable that he could not keep in check for long. Maybe the extremity of feeling we had seen on the stage quieted his own on that occasion. Maybe that is what the words of one great man do for another; though indeed Mr Hazlitt was shortly to prove himself a lesser.

26

After he had been peaceable and gracious and well-mannered with my mother to a degree that she might fancy herself the Queen of Sheba, the next thing was he came down and assailed her, and her family too. Maybe the influence of Romeo had been acting on his brain. His brain indeed never ceased to be active, play or no. But it seemed then to reach such a pitch it took a convulsion.

Of an evening some days after the play, we – that is, Mother, Cajah, Betsy and I – were gathered in the kitchen, which of all the apartments in the house is the only one we can call our own. And this also is the only time of the day we have a right to call ours, as the gentlemen do not make a habit of troubling us for their supper. We were just then in a more quiet and domestic mood than we are as a rule since Lizzie, who likes to make such a din with her clatter and talk, was out about the town on festive errands. My mother had set myself and Betsy to make a bachelor pudding for the Christmas table.

Mother is a jovial soul, and will not be stopped from talking. Now there we were, making a bachelor pudding – which, as is only natural in Mother, incited her to make remarks concerning the lodgers, who were nearly all of them bachelors. Excepting, indeed, Mr Hazlitt. And, carry on like a blushing boy in love though he could, he is surely as much a rake as the next man, or worse.

Thence she fell to ruminating on the general inclination in a bachelor to marry. She declared that she was not sure she could hold with the new ideal in proper manners that was coming in, that there should not be frankness of speech between a bachelor and the maid he is courting, nor any lipping or tickling either.

'I say a girl should see her man stripped before her wedding-night and content herself that he comes full-armed,' she said with a laugh.

'She should inspect him and make sure he has his full fig,' declared Cajah, to cap her argument.

Maybe this was not quite a proper thing to say in front of Betsy, who was assisting me in the pudding by scooping raisins up in a spoon. Martha would be certain to say so, and indeed to assert it was not proper that I should hear it either. But as Betsy attends the gentlemen nearly as much as I do – and why should she not since she would otherwise be idle – I am sure she has observed them in their differing states of undress as I have.

We may prefer to play at modern ladies and be spared the sight, but my mother is not one to see any sense in that. Anyway it is not our lot in life to be so delicate. And I can't see it doing any great harm to Betsy either. There is many a girl her age who must work in a factory from dawn to dark, and is privy in consequence to talk a great deal more coarse from men and women who are not even her own family.

Now we were embarked on Mr Griffith the Welsh-man. And Betsy, who found in him great comedy to laugh at, though I made sure to have as little to do with him as I could, left off licking her spoon and declared,

'If his trousers were to come down what a sight that would be.'

We all laughed at the prospect. And Cajah topped Betsy's remark with a bawdy one about the length of Mr Griffith's piece. Cajah is proud as punch of his own length, which he believes superior to the general run. I think as brothers and sisters we have a right to be frank as we choose on any matter, though a stranger might not find it refined in us. After all, they make a joke of my small pair in front, even Martha may when she is not too serious. And, as Cajah whipped out his piece often enough to show it off since he was a waddling little boy, it is no stranger to us.

'He is longer than Mr Follett, I am sure,' said Cajah.

And though none of us is as fanatic as my brother on the subject, for a laugh I put forward a new proposition. 'I say Mr Follett wears straps,' I said.

'What are straps?' queried Betsy.

'I have no need of straps,' answered Cajah, 'and from that information it must be plain to you what they are.'

Betsy put on a pout and said she knew what stays were and men wore them too, and she supposed straps were the same. That was enough talk of straps and stays, my mother announced then. And if we did not wish to be strapped, or stayed late from our bed, we might make haste with the pudding.

We fell silent and I commenced to stir the fruity mess in the basin. At that moment the door to the passage was burst open of a sudden. And who tumbled in among us but Mr Hazlitt, so urgent you could think he was fleeing from some monster at his heels. But he was not wan or pale as he should be from such a terror. His face was crimson and his eyes burning in fury so you might have thought to light a taper from them.

'Well? What would you say of me, then?' he shouted.

'Out with it. You have no shame in cackling at a man behind a closed door. Out with it in his presence, I say.'

He was marching about from one to the other of us, his mouth working with such a degree of temper that he could not get out his words. His spit flew in our faces.

'There is nothing we mean to say of you, I'm sure, Mr Hazlitt,' my mother stammered. Her face was as bloodless as his was the opposite.

'You lie, ma'am. And liar that you are, you are also shameless. You speak like a whore, ma'am. Is this a house of whores I am living in?'

My brother stepped forward, his hands patting the air to soothe the visitor – though he was one who had no right in the world to come visiting among us in the first place. 'Calm yourself, sir. I tell you we meant nothing . . .'

He could not finish his statement, as Mr Hazlitt seized a chair from its place by the table and pitched it upon the floor. It might have struck Cajah, and I believe Mr Hazlitt intended that it should, only his target jumped to the side and saved himself. Betsy, fearing for the pudding, took up the basin and, enfolding it fast in her arms, backed away into a corner. I could neither move nor speak a word. My power to breathe, my very heartbeat, seemed to have come to a stop. I was frozen as in a nightmare when the horror is invisible all around you, and the next moment will bring it into view.

Now he stepped up to me. He stood lowering before me and stared into my eyes with a hating look that I would have shrunk from into the earth if I were only able.

'I have called you an angel. Nay, a saint. A deity even . . .' Here he turned back to his audience, who were rooted to the spot as I was, like stone figures in the ground. 'I dare say it comes as no surprise to you that

143

she is but a slut. You who live with her know her for the little smiling seductress she is. But I never knew it until this night. Oh, I suspected it often enough . . . But I never did believe it before – though I had evidence enough for it . . .' He rocked his head in his hands in a show of stupefaction. 'Am I a fool? Am I indeed a fool?'

Turning to me again – 'Have you nothing to say? Have you no defence?' He seemed now to come to himself a little. There was a note of entreaty in his voice. 'Say something, Sarah. Say something, to cool me. You have cooled me often enough. You do not want for cooling words when we are in private together and you have put me in heat . . . Will you not say something now?'

Had I words to say, I would not have been able to utter them. My tongue, my lips, were all frozen, as was my heart to feel.

He took again the middle of the room and pointed to me as a judge points at the guilty one who is condemned to Bottomless or to hang. 'Do you know how excellent she is to heat up a man? What a little warming-iron she can be, and how easy, when she is alone in his room with a man? Yes, with her kisses and her soft arms twined about his neck? And she will do more than that if she is asked. But I am a fool and never asked it. But you, madam, will know what a little she-devil she can be. She has been well taught.'

My mother took sufficient offence from this, though she is not a body who is in general so inclined, to attempt to defend herself and me. 'Sarah is a good girl. And she may kiss whom she wishes, for I am sure a kiss now and then is no bad thing for a girl as long as she no more than kisses.'

As if in a reverie and talking to himself, Mr Hazlitt muttered, 'I dare say she has been kissing since she was a child.'

Waking, he pointed the finger at Betsy in her corner though she was almost lost behind the pudding-basin. 'The wench, young as she is, is kissing already, I dare say. And whomsoever she selects, since she does not want for teachers. Is Mr Griffith her victim? Or maybe it is Mr Tompkins? For there can be no objection to sharing one's favourites in a house such as this one . . . Might I next be favoured with a kiss or two?'

To hear herself singled out for contempt frightened Betsy to such a degree that she forgot herself. Or it might be that the pain Mr Hazlitt's words caused to her was greater than the ache growing in her arms as an effect of minding the makings of the pudding. The basin slipped from her grasp and with a great smash was shattered on the floor. At the noise, and seeing the pudding in a mess on the flags that had not been recent scrubbed, so it could not be saved, Betsy collapsed into loud sobbing. My mother, at last finding the power of her feet, went to her, and poor Betsy buried her sobs in her front, to be safe from the blazing sight of Mr Hazlitt.

'You have insulted my family and myself, Mr Hazlitt,' my mother protested. 'And here you have made my little daughter cry.'

Mr Hazlitt's rapt mute stare moved from Mother and the heaving figure of Betsy to arrive at me. His features began to work anew. 'What have I done?' he moaned. 'What have I done?'

Receiving no answer, he ran from the room. Still rooted in our positions, we listened to the stamp of his boots as he took the stairs two at a time. We heard the front door slam.

'Let him find his comfort in the street,' said my brother, after a long silence in which none of us could find a means to speak. 'He has no need of any of us to tell him what a whore is.'

Picking up the overset chair, he sat down in it, quite limp.

'You shall make a fresh pudding tomorrow,' my mother was telling Betsy.

'Well, if I do, he should be made to pay for it,' said Betsy through her teary gulps, though they now began to fall off a little.

'It was surely the devil himself who sent the man across our family peace,' exclaimed my mother, in a wailing voice near as bad as Betsy's.

I had the headache fit to die. But I could not think of going up the stairs to my bed for fear of meeting Mr Hazlitt or any of the other gentlemen – whether I had kissed them or no. I thought I should never leave the kitchen. But even that place did not seem safe as it had, since it was plain that any of them could come and listen at the door, on his way to or from the small-house, and burst in upon us to accuse us of whatever he fancied. We discovered ourselves to be speaking in low tones and without our usual habit of freedom.

'What will Mr Walker say if Mr Hazlitt leaves us?' fretted my mother, 'and in such a condition too that he is sure to hear of it. Indeed, he is a man to find out Mr Walker and insult him to his face as brazen as he has us. Mr Hazlitt is such a man for spite. I have always thought it.'

'I say we will be well shut of him if he goes.' My brother's defiance was returning, but I am sure he was no more keen for my father to hear of the fracas than was my mother.

'It is all on account of him being in love with Sarah,' said Betsy. 'He did not mean it, I am sure. But he had no right to blow me out.'

'He did not mean it,' echoed my mother, choosing to put forward the truth of that as a means of restoring some sign of order to the house. 'I believe he must be a little touched. But he had no right indeed to say any of it, whether he meant it or no. And no right to come prowling around the kitchen and eavesdropping at the door like a servant. I have always said it, he is not a gentleman.'

'No scribbler for the newspapers is a gentleman,' replied my brother. 'They find a better profession who are.'

'That is the last Irishman I will consent to have in the house,' declared my mother. 'A Welshman may make you laugh by his antics but an Irishman is sure to make you cry. My own mother always said it and now here is her proof.'

She warned me I must not encourage him any more and must withhold any kisses from him in the future. Then it would surely all blow over.

'I am sure he will not want them now,' I said.

'Oh, you may be sure he will,' said my mother. 'He is crazy as a plate. I can tell you he is that much in, he could not get out if he wanted. We are fortunate he is married. I'm sure, Sal, that if he were not, and were to offer himself to you for a husband, I would not let you take him. No, I am sure I would not. A man who shows as much temper as he has shown tonight is no fit husband for a girl of mine. There is nothing to match a peaceful house and a man who keeps out of rows. Look at your father. Look at Mr Roscoe. Can Mr Hazlitt stand in comparison with men such as they are?'

'But he intends to marry Sarah,' objected Betsy.

My mother looked sharp at me.

'He intends to go to Scotland and be divorced from his wife,' I cried out, my peril new borne in on me. 'He will hear of nothing but that I shall marry him on his return.'

My brother gave a low whistle. 'You're for the jump, then, Sal.'

'Lizzie will scrape up the pudding, I am sure,' mother murmured in a distracted fashion, as if this was the greatest trouble we were facing. 'Why, he might see sense after this and let his divorce be,' she allowed after a little – hopeful now despite what she had announced a minute before.

She could have had no notion that it had gone so far and Mr Hazlitt's fancies were to be given such substance. But her biggest fear was not for me, but for herself *vis-à-vis* Father. And so that he might not hear of it she told us that Mr Hazlitt should not be made to feel he was unwelcome in the house, but we should continue to attend him with the same consideration he had always enjoyed from us. As for me, she was decided that I should not be cold with Mr Hazlitt, nor warm either. 'He will surely be discouraged,' she said, 'if you keep your distance.'

'I should have no trouble in that,' declared Betsy. 'But I shall be civil with him all the same. He gives me a tanner when I do him a service. He is gone crazy but it is all on account of Sarah.'

27

For some days I dodged Mr Hazlitt, and never went near his room. This was not hard to manage since he was a great deal absent from the house, out of a sense of shame, I expect, and well merited too. When he was here, he was to be seen lingering in the passages the very picture of pain and dejection, and was asking after me from Betsy and Lizzie at every turn.

At last, when it could no longer be put off, I went to him.

I went with a resolve to be cold. I found him slouched over his table, and his fire black. A sentence was only half-formed on the page but he put down his pen and stood up to greet me. I no more than murmured a response.

'Are you angry with me?' he asked in quite a quavery way.

'There's a question now,' I said. 'I suppose I have no reason to be angry.'

His lower lip trembled. He turned away to hide it. 'Sarah,' he pleaded, when he had composed himself, 'did I not have some reason too for my conduct the other night?'

'Only what was your own doing.'

'That may be. But having heard what I did, can you not accept that I was troubled?'

'You had no right to listen to a private conversation.'

'Indeed I had not. But unless I misheard, and I do not believe I did, had I not a right to be angry?'

'I don't know what you heard.'

Of a sudden he was half-crazy again. Not as fierce, thanks be, as he had been in the kitchen, but sufficient to make me draw back and be grateful I had left the door ajar.

'To hear my angel, she to whom I imputed every virtue of innocence and sweetness, utter such obscenities . . .' His voice was rising in pitch. 'To be brought so brutally to the realisation that I could have had you, oh yes, Sarah, many a time, and shown you too as many inches as you could hope for . . . Only I thought you a dear good girl who would have none of it. A gentle creature who would consider herself dishonoured and defiled were I to so much as attempt it.'

Now he was marching about the room, one moment throwing me a pleading look, and the next a venomous. His lip curled. I knew I must be as careful with him as if we were engaged in a game of jackstraw.

'Was I wrong, Sarah? Would you rather be tickled and jumped like a kitchen-maid? Do I, with my mild caresses and my affectionate kisses, repel you? Is Mr Griffith or Mr Tompkins or indeed Mr Follett – who wears straps –' This last word he spat . . . 'Are these good gentlemen more vigorous than I? Do you discourse with them on my lovesick conduct? Do you laugh at me, together, for a fool and a sop? Tell me, Sarah. When you come to me in the mornings do you come after a lusty romp in Mr Tompkins' bed? And that is why you can appear so pure and faint? Do you come to me when you are sated? And that is how you are so well able to play the saint?'

I was fair alarmed to hear all of a sudden the name of Mr Tompkins brought into it. I made to go. He stepped brisk between me and the door.

'Let me go, sir,' I begged.

Now he changed his tune. 'I cannot. It is not in my power to let you go until I am forgiven. Forgive me, my own love — for you are that and will be always, no matter how much you may deceive me. Forgive me, I beg you, if you do not wish me mad. You have near driven me mad. I declare I am mad already. Mad with grief, for my angel, my gift, the one gift life has seen fit to grant me, and the dread of losing her. Only tell me, Sarah, that you are not callous, that you love me even a little. I beg you, tell me I am not quite deceived.'

I was resolved to be cold, to uncoil both him and myself from the tentacles of his hopes, which was the merciful thing. But he was so pitiful I all but weakened. And also I did not see why I should own to deceit, and thereby betray myself with a lie, as a means of relieving his suffering. But the truth might give him a hope I did not intend.

'Sir,' I began, attempting to choose my words with care, though I had not sufficient composure nor clarity to choose those I would like. 'Sir, you have no right to harass me as you do. I have never attempted to deceive you. I have told you from the start that my feelings for you could amount to no more than friendship.'

It was hard on me to say it, for I knew they would cause him anguish. But can love live on pity, or a girl's wish to please? And yet I dare say he would have asked for nothing more than that, he was so far gone. The colour in his face, which had heightened in hue as he grew frenzied, now left it.

'Why, then, do you kiss me?' he asked in a low dull tone. 'Why do you press yourself to me and twine your arms about my neck? Are you so easy that you consider such gestures a thing of nothing and will bestow them on any man?'

I could make no reply. How was I to explain to him the comfort a kiss could be in a life as comfortless as mine? That such gestures as he called them are but natural expressions of admiration and affection. How a girl in my position is used to them since she first buds and is pawed by the gentlemen – who would most of them be as much surprised to find she should read anything of great significance in them, as I was to find Mr Hazlitt did. It need not mean I wished to be his mistress or his wife. There had been a gentleman in whom I had placed such hopes, but I had learned not to hope any more. I did indeed love Mr Hazlitt, I am sure. But only in a little way. And of what use is such a little love as that to such a man?

'I have done no wrong, sir.' That was all I could assert. Whatever I had done, and I could see nothing very wrong in it, it was all his doing and at his bidding. I was hardly ever forward, but did only what he asked. Was it not he who twined my arms around his neck, until I became accustomed to it? Who seated me on his lap so it came to be a natural place of warmth and comfort? Why should he reproach me now for it? Why should a man expect a girl to be better than he is?

His face was softening. 'If you mean to say, by what you have just said, what I believe you to mean, you are not the character I feared you to be, Sarah. And there is yet hope for me.'

I, however, knew it was hopeless. There was nothing I could say, when he was in such a trance, to get him to see how he stood with me.

He had forgotten to keep the door and I seized my chance. I may be low-sized, but I am not a child and I do not see why I should go about in fear of anyone – least of all a man who was proposing to make me his wife. But I was unable to leave him in ignorance of the shame and anger he had caused to rise in me, and on the threshold I turned and remarked, 'I am obliged to you, sir, for letting me know the opinion you hold of me.'

In an instant he had fetched me back. 'I love you. That is the only opinion I hold concerning you. You cannot leave me . . . Give me a kiss at least, Sarah, before you go. You have never left me without a kiss when I asked it. And I have never wished so dear for your kisses as I do now.'

How was I to kiss a man to whom my kisses meant that I was only a wanton or a whore?

'Never,' I declared.

And then I was on the stairs.

28

His madness did not keep him from his work. When, after an interval in which I cooled and hoped he did, I next went to his room with his morning-tray, he had finished his story of the Fight. He begged that he might read it to me. I knew I should not give in to the request but I was weary of quarrels and confusions and thought I might humour him in this matter at least.

As I sat and listened, I thought again how fine he wrote and that I might esteem him again in the old way if he would not coerce me.

'Now,' he said, as he came towards the finish, and looked up at me from his foolscap with a look of sadness, but satisfaction too, 'here is where I have put you in.'

I started up. 'I do not wish to be written of.'

'Oh, you are not visible in it,' he assured me. 'You would never recognise yourself in the reference, nor would anyone else. It is but a little message to myself, such as a writer likes to indulge in now and then.'

And a message also to your friends, I wanted to say. But I did not wish to incite another quarrel.

' "Though I am bitter as coloquintida",' he read, and looked at me significant again . . . 'You see, it is you have made me bitter. I would not have written that were it not for you. But I shall be sweet again by and by, shall I not, Sarah?'

I felt the injustice of it but I could make no reply. 'Well, you could not write in such a lively manner if you were truly bitter as coloquintida,' I might have said. Whatever that substance is, I suppose it is something frightful sour, like a physic. But I have no power of expression, even were I free to talk back to such a man. A girl has not the pleasure of free speaking.

'What is coloquintida?' I enquired, to turn him off from the topic. He said that, why, as was plain from what he wrote, it was a bitter substance, leaving me none the wiser.

I told him then that his article was very fine. He agreed that indeed it was and he could hope to get a fine fee for it.

'I shall need as much money as I can gather for my trip to Scotland.' He looked at me with meaning.

'I dare say Scotland is a dear place,' I parried, as if I did not know nor care for what reason he was travelling to that country.

I wished he would not continue to look for a divorce. However, I was contented with telling myself that he understood at last it was not on my account. I had spoken as plain as a girl can about the true state of my feelings and he could not be deluded any more on that subject, except in so far as he chose. He was going off to Scotland with the purpose of freeing himself from a wife he did not love. I was no longer a part of the bargain. It was a general freedom from her he was buying, as a man might buy himself out of the army when he was grown tired of the discipline and the fighting. I need have no place at all in it, I reasoned. After all, does a soldier go to great expense to get out of his regiment only to sign up for another, and a fresh rout? Where such a man knows he is not made for the military, Mr Hazlitt knows he is not made for marriage. I neglected to consider that a soldier is likely to be a man of sense, while Mr Hazlitt, being a man of letters, was likely to be either mad or foolish.

Now that I had returned to his room and we sat together again rather in our old easy way – for to be peaceful is surely for the best and always worth a little compromise – I was wary, you can be sure, and on the watch for any signs in him of untoward passion or imminent phrensy. We were then in the early days of the new year of 1822 – and before very long now it will be 1824. What a time has passed since. And yet it is a short time in comparison with the length of my life – that is, if I am not granted the good fortune of blowing out from shame before my natural span.

Mr Tompkins was not yet returned from his Christmas in Liverpool, nor was the Welshman returned from Wales, and I had little work to do – but even less to amuse or divert me, though I was often free to do as I pleased. My mother had given up discouraging me from passing an hour or two with Mr Hazlitt, though I am sure she might have if only she had foresight.

'I am glad to see you are friends again,' she said. 'We would not want the trouble we had before. It would disturb the gentlemen when they return. And, besides, 'twould give great annoyance to your father if he thought we could not run the house without that kind of trouble.'

Her principal purpose was to keep Mr Hazlitt soothed and calm in case his tantrum should come to my father's attention. Would she have been so indulgent if Mr Hazlitt were not a man of repute? Well, I believe she would, as my mother is a woman who chooses to consider a lodger to be in general in the right. Downstairs we must labour under the burden of whatever trouble they may bring. In this way she keeps her excellent name as a roomkeeper and will never be short of a lodger – while we may lose our names, for all she cares. But since she does not design it, I suppose she is hardly to be blamed.

Mr Hazlitt's conduct was so tender and his manner so rueful that I could not but forgive him and some of my former affection for him was restored. He had not after all lost his power of discourse and the time passed as rapid in his company as ever it was used to. I found, however, that I was near as silent as I was in the first days of our acquaintance. I no longer reposed a great deal of confidence in him, fearing his misunderstandings and his elevated standards regarding a girl's words and her actions. He spoke of his coming sojourn in Scotland as no more than a nuisance, a trifling duty that would be soon accomplished. After it was done, he said, he would go away to Italy on his tour of that country's famous sights, which he had spoken of before.

'It will be a great expense,' I ventured, troubled that he owed my father a term's rent and yet would take on himself the cost of travel when he also had the price of his divorce to think of.

'Colburn has agreed to send me to Italy,' he said, 'and is ready to pay me well for the results.'

He often made the claim that this publisher or that would be passing on great sums to him. A hundred guineas for this, five hundred for that – and yet he had frayed sleeves to his shirts and owed his rent. So I had no cause to believe him now.

He took my hand and placed it on his knee and stroked it. 'But what would Italy be, with all her beauties, and what could it mean to me without my little Cockney love at my side?' he murmured.

His words as always gave me some little delight, though indeed I should not have taken pleasure in them, since I know now that they were neither idle nor calculated. I let him keep possession of my hand, though neither should I have.

'Sarah?' he said, in the low voice that let me know the manner of my response meant a great deal to him, 'Would you come with me to Italy? If you could come honourably?'

By this, I am sure, he intended to say 'as Mrs Hazlitt'. He did not dare to say it for fear that I would turn cold. Appearing not to mind that I made no answer, he went on to paint a picture of Italy as a fine place full of history, with an antique ruin at every turn, all bathed gold in a sun whose tincture and strength we in England know nothing of. But Italy, I think, though it may possess more than its quota of picturesque ruins, is a wild, barren place where brigands roam. And its strong sun is not kind to the English complexion, nor its stagnant waters healthy for the English constitution. I should soon myself be a picturesque ruin to match its own were I to go there, I thought.

Seeing him musing on his dreams in his rapt manner, and on my countenance, which does not please me, I turned my head away so he had only my profile, which is better, to consider.

'And on the way to Italy, there is France to be explored,' he continued. 'That has its own beauties. We might inspect Vevey and the rocks of Meillerie and all the places Rousseau wrote of.'

Rousseau, the French writer, was a great favourite of his and he had promised me before a volume of his works. However, he had never presented it, so I had no means of picturing for myself the beauties of Vevey nor the vaunted rocks of Meillerie.

'Do you say you will consider at least coming to Italy with me, Sarah?' he insisted.

I feared he was become too intent on it. If I were to assent he was likely to throw himself upon me in a phrensy of joy. While if I refused he would surely burst out in a phrensy of the other sort. To be neutral was the best way of answering that I could see. 'I do not know,' I replied.

His countenance took on a look of dejection. But he was not quite despairing and I felt myself safe. Fearing more persistent discussion on the subject, I rose and went, knowing I had escaped in no bad degree from committing myself too far – while saving him from too great a hope, or its opposite.

29

Now it was his last night with us before his departure for Scotland. I did not approve of his mission but neither did I want him to leave in a state of disarray or without bidding him farewell. I went to his room to assist in the packing of his things, though indeed they were so scanty I was scarce needed.

He would not be still but wandered about the room, picking up a book and putting it down again, and oversetting his few pieces of dress that I had folded neat. I was irked and wished I had not come.

When he spoke, it was in a kind of reverie half to himself, on nonsensical subjects I had no wish to hear. Where were he and his love to live? By a mountain or a lake? Perhaps by them both. And they were to take not only their breakfast together but their dinner and supper too . . . Next he wondered whether his marriage bed should face the window, as the Hindoos place it, or the door, as in his mother's house. And he assured me that he would insist she wore her mob-cap when they travelled in the coach together, for she was prettiest in her mob-cap, though he knew she did not think so . . .

Altogether he seemed to me like a man who had once a dream that was precious to him, but now it was vanished and he knew it to be so. Growing reasonable, he asked me to forgive him for his fancies since as yet he had no right to them. And I was not quite as well disposed to him yet as I might . . . though soon I could be.

'Shall I not have a right to my fancies when I return from Scotland?' he pleaded. 'Shall I find you receptive to them then?'

'You shall find me the same,' I answered.

I was proud of my prudent answer and left him. However, as I lay in bed, I was distracted by the thought of my coldness towards a man who was so often kind, and was sorry for it. And was only able to sleep by resolving that a token of affection as he went off need not be imprudent, nor get me into a scrape. Any man, after all, is in need of a word of encouragement from his friends as he sets out on a journey, in particular when he goes as far as Scotland.

The next morning, before I had gone up to him, word came down from Cajah that Mr Hazlitt wished to see my mother. I was surprised he had not summoned me. She went – and in a short while tumbled in on us in a state of great confusion.

'He is not coming back,' she exclaimed. 'He is emptying his room. What will Mr Walker say? He will be grieved that we let him go. And we may well be cut out of the business if his friends are told he was not happy with us. They are to come for his pictures and his little statue. We shall be obliged to take in a low class of lodger. What will your father say? He is so fond of Mr Hazlitt living with us.'

'He is not leaving us,' I said. 'He is only going on a journey. He is going to Scotland.'

'He is indeed going to Scotland. But on his return he will not be coming back to us. We are to mind his things only until Mr Patmore calls for them. And then we may let his rooms or not as we wish . . .

'Sal,' she cried then in her wheedling way that I am unable to turn away, 'You must go to him. You must persuade him not to leave us. He will not find better lodgings in the whole of London. You must tell him so. Your father thinks him as good as ten lodgers. Why, he would keep him for nothing, only I will not allow it. Go up now direct and find a means to make him stay.'

I own I was upset too to think that he could leave us so sudden – and after all his declarations to me. Either he did not love me from morning till night after all, as he claimed, or he was in a pique and would be despairing until I consoled him. My feelings of friendship for him were such that they would not let me see him despair. And now here was my mother wishing it too. I went up.

He was cool and seemed resigned to the loss of both his hopes and his rooms. I saw that the picture he used to venerate as my likeness was taken down and stood, the vacancy of its back turned out, against the wall.

Requesting me to sit and talk a little with him, his manner was absent, like a man's towards a younger sister who is of little account, or perhaps the girl who attends to him and for whom he holds a certain affection, but nothing stronger. After his fancies of the night previous it was perhaps silly in me to think it – but I am modest as that and have such little faith in a man's protestations. Yet in truth it challenged me into seeking to regain some little power over him. A girl does not like to be dropped so easy.

He spoke as if our friendship were now in the past.

'You were fond of me once, were you not, Sarah? When I came first to the house you sat with me very contented and you were affectionate towards me.'

But he did not sigh or sulk or make any pleas as he was used to – indeed, as he had so late as the night before.

'Why was that, Sarah? Maybe I reminded you of someone?'

I was at a loss. 'Remind me of someone? I do not think so.'

'Of a lover, perhaps? One you still think of?'

'Oh no,' I said. 'You are not at all like anyone I ever knew. But there is one who is.'

'Who is that?'

'Your little man.' I did not mind telling him, now that he was going away. He was confused. I looked at the little man where he stood on the mantel. 'That little image resembles someone I once knew.'

'Do you mean my Napoleon?' And he laughed, a good and proper laugh, unlike the dry and meaning laughs he was wont to make of late. 'And your friend's figure, was it the same?' he enquired.

'No. He was taller. And not as stout.'

In an instant he had placed the little man in my hands to hold.

'And he has a fairer complexion,' I continued.

And Mr Hazlitt laughed again, quite hearty, for the little image was fashioned out of a bronze-coloured lustre. 'Take him,' he said, 'take him off with you. Patmore was to come for him. But since you are so fond of him you shall keep him.'

Now I was confused indeed. Mr Hazlitt wished to give me the possession he favoured most in the world – and the action gave me new doubt that he had ever loved me. If he loved as he said, he could not be happy to see me go off clutching the image of someone else next to my heart. His protestations were only a front to induce me into indiscretions and his sufferings were all feigned. I had the sensation that everything was turned around, that it was I who loved and I who would be melancholy and all alone when he was gone. I was no better than my mother, I did not wish him to leave us for good, nor him to picture me, without it affecting him in the least, pining over the image of Mr Bradley in my chamber.

'I shall take him,' I said, 'but only to guard for you, sir, and to keep safe until your return.'

It may have been wrong of me, I own, to make such a presuming declaration. But the look of delight that softened his features out of their assumed carelessness relieved me. He was not changed towards me after all. His delight was transparent, like a child's at finding his cherished spinning-top after it was lost. And I knew he would soon come running back to us like a child frightened by the streets.

Now I did a thing I had never done, as I was never the first to go to him before. I took his hand in mine and placed his about my neck and kissed him. For I was fond of him and grateful. A girl may kiss her old friend, surely, in the way he has often kissed her, especially now he was going off on a long journey to another country.

Tender again as ever he was, he could hardly bear to tear himself from my arms. Nor indeed was I eager as I had been to see him go.

'Last night I thought of tearing it off,' he murmured when I played with the chain bearing the golden heart with the coil of my hair in, which hung still about his neck. 'I feared you had grown cold to me. You know, I was almost accustomed to the idea. Though in truth I believe I could not have borne it. Now I shall go to Scotland the happiest of men.' He buried his head in my front, sighing with the renewal of his hopes.

I do not believe I was seeking to deceive. I ensured only that he went off happy. He did not attempt to extract any promises from me – and if he had I would not have given any. However, he is the kind of man to fancy promises where there are none. That has nothing to do with me. I do not see that I should calculate my actions at every turn for fear of someone taking them up wrong. Is a man to be allowed to be natural and spontaneous as he wants, and a girl never? That is what they would like, for us to be governors and maids and children and politicians all at once, as well as who knows what else – this is what they call a lady.

But it is hard to be a lady with never a holiday from it. I do not believe even a regular lady can manage it. A lady, it seems to me, wears fetters as tight and painful as what a poor wretch wears on his way to Bottomless. Only he is better off as he will be rid of them once he is landed there, as long as he is still in one piece.

'Old Hazlitt had a jaunty step as he went up the street,' observed Cajah, meeting me on the stairs. 'Has he made good his escape? Or is he in deeper than ever he was?'

I hurried off from him to the kitchen.

'Well?' asked my mother. 'Have we lost him?'

'I believe he will come back,' I said.

She laughed. 'Our Sal has a great way with the gentlemen, and no mistake.'

'Look out that one of these days she does not have too great a way,' put in Lizzie.

'Sally knows how to mind herself, and that is more than we can say for some,' retorted Mother, riled by this impudence from Lizzie, who has little entitlement to talk on that subject.

Cajah came in. 'Well, well,' he announced, 'I see she has his itty Boney on the mantel in her room. Have you taken to pilfering, Sal?'

'He gave it to me to mind for him,' I said stiff, 'until he comes back.'

'So he is more fond of her than he is of his fat little

chaynie fellow who he thinks so precious.' Cajah made a low whistle.

I left them and went to sit in the parlour under the lamp with Mr Hazlitt's book. My mother did not complain.

30

A few days after his departure I received a letter from Mr Hazlitt. It did not please me; indeed, on the contrary. It was passing frank and effusive. He spoke of my loving tenderness on the day he took his leave of me, that his heart was singing at the memory and he was kept warm by it though the fields without were frosty and his fire would not draw as it did when I stoked it . . . The trees were bare, he wrote, but he found them more beautiful than in the spring when they would be clothed in green. 'They are as you will be, Sarah, when we are together in that state which I have reason to believe you too begin to consider blessed . . .'

I was vexed and shamed. Had I not made plain to him my reluctance to hear him speak, let alone write, on that subject? And he had not stopped to think that my family would wish to peruse a letter I received from him, we do not get so many letters that one is not a source of interest. I was obliged to put it at once in the flames – which, I declare, were no hotter than my ears were upon reading it.

In the evening I had further reason to be ashamed. His friend Mr Patmore called on us. This is the man Mr Hazlitt put into his story of the Fight, but in an excellent and generous light of course, since Mr Patmore is a gentleman and not a tradesman's daughter.

Mr Patmore demanded, with a special kind of smile that Cajah mimicked when he came down to fetch me, to see Miss Walker – the Miss Walker 'who is a special friend of Mr Hazlitt's'. With no small degree of reluctance, for I was flustered that Mr Hazlitt had spoken of me outside the house, I went to meet him. He was a ruddy personage, with hair a bright mahogany colour, kept up, I am sure, by Atkins's dye.

'You wish to see me, sir?' I asked, as polite as I could, though I did not extend my hand.

Mr Patmore inspected me as if I were a commodity of no great price on sale in a shop. 'Well,' he said after a little, as if deciding against the purchase after all, 'you have been a great distraction to my poor friend. I hope you will agree to be kinder by and by, when he returns.'

'You come on an errand, sir?' I said, quite cold.

'I have come to take away Mr Hazlitt's picture. The one that is your likeness, I believe.'

Cajah went to fetch it down. When it was presented to Mr Patmore he appraised the figure with the same curiosity that he had me.

'So this is his Myrrha,' he said at last and gave a dry laugh. 'A man when he is in love has strange fancies.'

On the next day I wrote to Mr Hazlitt to tell him that his picture was now safe in Mr Patmore's keeping. And that I did not care at all about its removal and it could stay where it was as far as I was concerned, if they would agree to talk of it and not of me. Not that I expressed anything of the kind in words, but if Mr Hazlitt were a sensible man he would understand it was what I wished to say. I also hoped his writing was going on well – meaning by this that he should not waste his time in writing letters to me that would only be put on the fire.

I wrote in the cool and formal manner that comes

most natural to me – though no manner of writing does come natural in truth. In any case it would be shaming to attempt to express myself in any other way to a person who is able to express his self with the same ease that a bird sings. I hoped he might see this was the style of writing I preferred in a letter, and that he should confine himself to the same style in his missives if he wished to save me from shame and keep my friendship.

But the next letter he wrote was near as expressive as the first and I left off hoping he might ever understand me. And yet I did not destroy it but kept it hidden in the bottom of the chest under my petticoats, for it was more affectionate in tone than passionate, and I thought it suggested he might not insist on having me for a wife but could accept me as a friend when he came back.

In it he informed me he had made it safe as far as Scotland and was staying at the Renton Inn in Berwickshire. I had fancied him to be in the Highlands with only bannocks and mutton to eat – though indeed that fare would suit him well enough. But since he spoke of smacks sailing in the bay I decided he must be by the sea.

He was writing ten pages a day at the Inn, which is more, I am sure, than he ever wrote when he was with us. Mr Patmore had the right of it, I dare say, in considering me a distraction. He boasted that this rate of production, if he kept it up, would amount to earnings of thirty guineas a week. Now, let me say concerning this subject that, if I was concerned only with money and gifts, as he has written in his book, would I not have married him at once for his thirty guineas a week? Why he should pretend I was interested in his money, or any man's, I don't know.

And again he wrote in that letter of what no gentleman should – 'the thousand endearing caresses that have passed between us'. If my brother had got wind of that he would never be done throwing it at me and extracting favours of one kind or another for keeping it secret. Also, he wrote that he wished to be my 'proud and happy slave'. No girl, I am sure, believes in that kind of sweet talk, for, as my mother was fond of saying, it cannot last beyond a week when you are man and wife.

As for Mr Tompkins, I thought then that I should die if he were to read such shaming effusions as these. He was due to return to us any day now, from Liverpool. But after all, it is astonishing what you can endure, and still go on living, even if you have no wish to live, when the thing that you fear most comes to pass.

In the same letter, Mr Hazlitt offered tickets to Mother and me for the plays. We should see Mr Kean, he said, who was his favourite, in *Othello*, and Miss Stephens in *Love in a Village* and the Indian Jugglers, and what else I don't know. But I did not wish to be under any obligation to him and it would be only a trouble to my mother, who would not leave her place by the fire to go out and see swallowers of carving-knives or performances on the rope, even had I the desire to go. I don't believe I ever mentioned it to her.

I might have liked, I own, to go with Mr Tompkins. I would not have cared if it was to see the worst actors in the world strutting about the stage, as long as I saw them in his company. But that would not be at all proper. In any case I would prefer that such an invitation should come from Mr Tompkins himself, for then it would have meaning.

There was nothing in the way of business in the letter that demanded a reply. And that was fortunate, because, after a meeting I had with Mr Roscoe, I determined never to correspond with Mr Hazlitt again.

Mr Roscoe was in the habit of passing on to me the magazines to read. Soon after that, when I was at the

Roscoes', before he retired for his smoke he called me aside and handed me the *New Monthly* for February. 'Here is something written by Mr Hazlitt. Your sister thinks you should see it,' he said, with a grave but kind look. 'Look, there, where she has underlined.'

In an essay of Mr Hazlitt's printed in the magazine for all to see, I recognised for the first time, but not for the last, unlucky creature that I am, myself.

'Shouldst thou ever, my Infelice, grace my home with thy loved presence, as thou hast cheered my hopes with thy smile, thou wilt conquer all hearts with thy prevailing gentleness and I will show the world what Shakespeare's women were . . .' But lest anyone fancy he meant to honour me by those honeyed words, he went on to speak of the 'humble beauties' he preferred, among which it was clear that I was numbered – indeed, was the prime representative.

It was the first sign that he felt free to bandy my character about, not only in London but in all England where folk read the magazines. I was no more than meat to feed his musings. Indeed, perhaps I represented only the few shillings extra he would get for his lines. But people love to gossip of the affairs of writers and their frailties and they would harry at the bone until they found out who it was that Bill Hazlitt was tearing his hair over, and who it was that was putting him in a state like a lovesick poet. As Mr Patmore looked me over, so would the gentlemen as I passed the Inns. 'There goes Hazlitt's humble beauty . . .' 'It is she he has selected to sit at his board for his wife has grown as stale to him as a week-old loaf . . .' 'Is she worth the price of a divorce, do you say? . . .'

Martha came down from seeing my niece to bed. 'Well?' she said. 'Do you like to see yourself in print?' I fancied that she wore a kind of half-smile. 'Do not lecture me,' I instructed her. 'I am cross enough with myself, though it was none of it my doing.'

'You may have reason to be cross, I am sure. But it is a respectable reference he makes. And you cannot be recognised in it. But if you are, there is no harm in it. It is not uncomplimentary.'

'Give up the topic, I beg you,' I said. 'I cannot endure to be notorious or spoken of.'

She considered me a little, as if she would like to say more. However, I remained silent, and she took up her needle and turned the talk to something else. I was consoled enough by her accepting manner to believe my situation was in no particular peril; and was foolish enough to think I could stem the damage by stopping from any further correspondence with Mr Hazlitt. He would be a long time absent in Scotland and would surely find some humble beauty there to hook his attentions. For they are two a penny there, and red-headed too, and freckled enough for any poet. He must surely I thought, come back to London cooled.

31

His next letter came in March. His hand covered three or four pages. Lucky it was that no one saw it come. I put it aside for two days until I chose to read it. When I did, I was glad to find he was still at the Renton Inn, which indeed led me to hope some humble Scots maid in that place was in receipt of the heat of his affection. He had understood my letter well enough, for he apologised for having written in the crude way he had. But he was still so rash and unrestrained he could not stop from repeating the error.

He put down such things as he thought pertinent. And what were they? An account of the cook's court-night at Renton Inn was one. What did he think I should find of interest in the kitchen doings of an inn in Scotland that I should never know, or persons in it that I should never meet? He referred to private matters that had passed between us in such a way as to make me glad that no eyes but mine were reading of them. Now he has done it again so all the world may read.

There was a portrait of himself as a boy, he said, in his mother's house. And he wished to be told whether he had permission to send it to me – for he was sure I was the means to restore him to the innocence depicted in it. I understood by that that he wished to repose in me the ideals that Boney his Emperor, and his politics, and his irregular life, had robbed him of. So I was to be sweet and gentle and incapable of anger and would as a matter of course welcome anything he chose to throw at me.

But what was most offensive was that he put a postscript in which he spoke gay of Mr Patmore, making it plain that gentleman was privy to all the ups and downs of our case. By this he let me know quite plain that what was private between us two was raked over as he and his chums chewed their mutton-chops – or, worse, that he was writing it out in his missives to Mr Patmore. And if he blabbed it to Mr Patmore, who was but a recent acquaintance, how many more would he blab to?

'I love you and die for you,' he wrote. Well, it is not he who dies but I.

He wished to be remembered to all 'at home'. He could not see that this could be done only by letting them know I had received such a letter. Bound up in his own concerns and sensations, he was incapable of giving a moment's thought to mine. My father would grant Mr Hazlitt the wisdom a child grants its father. But Betsy is less childish than he is. I think he has no more than the wisdom of a babe who bawls and makes a noise to be given what it wants.

At about this time, Mr Tompkins returned to town and took up his rooms again. He was busy over his books and appeared preoccupied. But on a day in the middle of the month when it was passing fair for so early in the Spring, he took me walking along the Strand.

I found myself uncommon shy with him, for he struck me as even more handsome than he was wont, and his figure so very fine now that he was not covered up in his greatcoat and wore his new pair of Wellington boots. He mused as we went along about his family and the sacrifices a man must make when he has responsibilities and but a small competence. I supposed he was referring to his numerous sisters. Even were they well placed to work in the lodging-house trade and earn their independence, they could not, I knew, since they were ladies. I was sorry for him.

'Well, perhaps I shall show that a man need not be obliged to make a sacrifice, if he is diligent enough,' he decided at last. He was more cheerful then and smiled down on me and invited me into the Southampton to take some coffee. I agreed, but I continued to be downcast as a result of his former mood and when I was met with the hubbub of talk and the clatter of pots my courage failed me. When I begged him to take his coffee with his colleagues and let me go on, as my mother was waiting on me, he refused to enter on his own and came with me as far as Chancery-lane.

Mr Tompkins knew not to oppress a girl with dizzy talk and meaning looks. From these little considerations of his I knew he had a deal of regard for me. This implicit regard I valued ten times above Mr Hazlitt's reckless and old-fashioned declarations. Mr Hazlitt's enthusiasts might fancy I should be delighted to receive them, but, in my opinion, only an old maid of thirty could be. In these times a girl prefers restraint and decorum. Mr Hazlitt is all out of kilter in the present time.

His next correspondence was but a note. He was now arrived in Edinburgh and wished me to know it, so I might appreciate the lengths he was going to for my sake – though it was in reality all to serve his own fancies. He had adopted a light tone now, as if this might touch me where his tragic one had not. He gave mention to the money he owed my father for his lodgings, a sum of ten pounds. Intending to be back in London shortly, he would call on us to pay it.

Knowing my father would never press him for payment, I saw no necessity for replying. It was a delicate matter and best left to my mother – not to speak of what he was wishing me to say on my own account. I am unable to express myself on such matters. In any case, I did not wish to see him in London just then. The idea of he and Mr Tompkins under our roof, and he running up and down the stairs that was also used by Mr Tompkins, and watching me and questioning me, was more than I could bear.

No further word came from him then. In consequence I was not incited by his indiscretions, and it was not his moods and his pleadings I remembered, but engaged in fancies that he might be reconciled with his wife and would write a great book that not even his enemies, like John Bull, could pull down. In later years, I told myself, I would be able to say to anyone who spoke of him, 'Once he lived with us, and had a tender regard for me.'

He does not believe I ever had such a regard for him, though I had; nor loved him when he was at his best and not mad, though I did. Yet, I could never have married him – and especially not now that he was mad.

Maybe, I sometimes thought, he got pleasure in his love-sickness. And if I did consent to marry him, he would be cured of it and be no more content than he was with his wife. After all, he was so inclined to extremes that if he loved me now as he asserted, before very long his feelings must swing the other way and I might wake up one day and find myself hated. He was a man no woman could rely on.

'Mr Hazlitt is consistent in his opinions. That is a virtue,' declared Mr Roscoe more than once.

That need not mean he has the virtue of consistency in his affections. No, it means that amid the storm of his emotions that blow east and west, north and south, like the winds, his opinions are the one constant he holds fast to. Was he not always falling out with his friends? He fell out with Mr Wordsworth and Mr Coleridge in his youth. And now that he is elderly, he has more enemies than has any man in London. He made no true friend in our house apart from me, and then he had to make me out to be more than I was. He is a man who loves indeed – but he may be one who, once he wins his object's love, is repelled by it.

For all his fine words and his sermons, he has little understanding of human nature and lacks sympathy for our human weaknesses. Mr Hazlitt has replaced his idea of God that he once believed in but has lost, with a row of little gods. Boney was one. I was another. Well, he ought first to be godly himself. By his seeking to impose high standards on us he is no better than a churchman got up in black and frowning down upon his flock.

32

At least in Mr Hazlitt's absence, I was free to think about Mr Tompkins. The spring was come on, late, but sweet when it did. I left off my worsted gown and exchanged my thick mantle for my shawl. But I regretted to a degree the lengthening days, though I had always liked them before, because when he came home in the evening there was no necessity any more for me to light him up to his room with his candle. Still, I arranged my hair and my dress to be becoming and listened for his step, which I recognised at once, on the stairs. I was able in general then to find some pretext for exchanging a few light words with him. He never did come out with it express, but he let me know by his welcome and his looks that he waited too on my appearance – and that made me wish all the more for the words to be uttered.

On occasion he would ask for some light supper to be brought up. While he drank his cocoa I would turn down his bed and brush his coat in readiness for the morrow. Then he would push his cup away and pull me to him. Such scrapes as I got into then, seated on his lap and playing with his hair, that is near as fine as Baby's was, and he muzzling my neck. I declare we were for all the world like two nags in harness who are passing fond of each other.

One morning as I was leaving him, he stayed me. I had thought for some days that he did not look so rosy as he did once and feared London and his responsibilities were weighing on him. Now he said as much himself.

'Should you like to take the air this afternoon, Sarah? I find I am fagged for want of an outing. I am forward in my books so need not worry on that score, today at least.'

'An hour or two can do no harm, sir,' I said, and we arranged to meet at two o'clock outside the Crown and Anchor when he would have eaten his dinner. I got off mine by pleading the headache and insisted to Mother that a stroll in the Park would suit me better, as the trees were putting on their green cloaks.

'Yes – unlike the ladies, who are taking theirs off,' said Cajah.

When I promised I would eat a twopenny bun on my bench I was let off.

'Shall we walk towards Saint Paul's?' suggested Mr Tompkins. 'I have never looked inside the famous edifice.'

Nor had I indeed, though I could not care in what direction I went as long as I was with him. After a little, he took from his pocket some sticks of Spanish liquorice and barley-sugar and shared them with me. 'You know, I should like to offer you better gifts than penny sweets, Sarah,' he said with a rueful laugh. 'But this is as much as I can do just now.'

'I like them as well as any,' I protested.

A waif accosted us, doffing his stoved-in hat, and begged to be given a penny for victuals. He was content with a liquorice in lieu and then on my insistence Mr Tompkins had another and that was the last.

After the noisy pavements and brick walls of the

thoroughfare, the near-empty cathedral was vast and cool, done most elegant as it is in marble and stone. Mr Tompkins was quite impressed and wandered about with his head in the air declaring there was not a sight to match it in Liverpool or in all of England, he was sure, even if it was rather ornate for the English taste. Well, I felt near as happy as if I had built the echoing place myself for his pleasure. He would have liked to inspect it all from the vaults up to the ball. But as the levies were so steep we were confined to visiting the whispering gallery, which was twopence. It would have cost him two and eightpence for the whole show, and twice that if he had to pay for me.

As I grew tired he drew me down to rest in a pew which by chance was behind a pillar and out of the view of other visitors. And there he stole a kiss, though a chaste one, seeing as we were in a church. If his hand strayed, it was but a little, as I am sure any young man's must in such a circumstance. 'It is fortunate we are in a place of divinity,' he murmured most tender in my ear, 'else I believe I might eat you up.'

I was a distraction to him. A day or two after this, he came to tell my mother that he was leaving us. There was a distant relation of his who kept a house in Tooks Court, and now his father had written to say that this lady had a chamber empty and it would be both an economy and kinly if he were to take it. He was to repair there at once.

'I hope we have not neglected you, Mr Tompkins,' asked my mother, who was quite chagrined by his decision.

'On the contrary,' he replied. 'And indeed I do not intend to give up my happy connection with the house, even if I must leave you.'

Next he sent for me and informed me of his departure afresh. When he asked me to help him pack his box, I felt a tear starting to my eyes and could not keep it back. On seeing my sad looks, he took me into his arms and said that indeed it was better that he should go, for we would not be compromised any more when he lived at Tooks Court. It was hard by and we still could meet as often as he was able, and that would be near as often as we met here. He did not intend to break off our friendship, he assured me, even if he was going to his cousin's.

I believe that what he meant to say was, we had been thrown too much together in our house, and that was not proper. But once we were no longer under the same roof we might make our arrangements like a regular couple. Seeing as this was what he meant, I did not mind his leaving us in the least but considered it indeed an excellent thing – and with a joyful heart fell to packing his box. As I did, while he passed me articles to fold, he said something that encouraged me all the more.

'I hope you will be able to address me as Henry,' he said, 'when I shall be no longer a lodger in the house.'

'I will, and with pleasure,' I told him.

Just as Henry did not oppress me with his feelings, neither did he press me as to the strength of mine, except by these little means. I hate to be troubled by such questions. My opinion is that they ought to remain submerged like the stones that, when the sun shines, have a gemmy radiance, or the small silvery creatures that glint beneath the water in the pond in Regent's Park. If you fish them up to examine them, you find they are poor dull leaden things, or gasp for air if they are living, and the best you can do for them is return them to their own remote and murky regions where they can shine out again.

All this time Mr Hazlitt's friend Mr Patmore was calling every other week on some pretence. He wished to know if we had rooms to let, whether Mr Griffith was still with us, and such impertinences. What business was it of Mr Patmore's whether rooms of ours were engaged or no and to whom? If I had not had the chance to retire or go out, as he was arriving, he would take the opportunity of appraising me in his insolent way. Next he might suggest I was 'a little downcast today'. This was on account, perhaps, of my missing 'a certain person'?

He came only to spy on us, of course, on behalf of that 'certain person'. We saw quite clear what he was about but were civil with him – though in the kitchen we had our jokes to entertain us at his expense. Cajah could do a fine imitation of his sly enquiries and his leers.

On his last visit, Mr Patmore informed me that he believed Mr Hazlitt was expected back to town, and wished to know whether this news pleased me. I replied that, if it pleased Mr Hazlitt, my feelings on the matter were of no consequence.

In the middle of May there was a note come for my mother. Told it was from Mr Hazlitt, she gave it to me to read out. It was to say he would be with us on the Friday and trusted his rooms would be ready.

'Mercy,' she said, turning the letter this way and that, as if to judge his mood from it across his sobriety of manner. 'What are we to expect from him? Do you say he has cooled, Sally? Or will be of a mind to make trouble? Does he say he has his divorce? Or has he forgotten it? Let us hope he has forgotten it and will conduct himself as a gentleman . . .'

After a deal more of this kind of talk, which was but to reassure me, I believe, that she was on my side in the business, she arrived at the conclusion that this was his home and he would be made welcome in it. But we, and I in particular, were to be no kinder to him than to any other lodger. For my part, I must have been living then in a fool's paradise. I reasoned that, even had my father and mother been content to turn him away from his home for my sake, there was the old tie between us that prevented me from depriving him of it.

I prepared his rooms, just as I might for the return of any of our gentlemen. And I returned the little image of Bonaparte to its place on the mantel, hoping he would understand by this that I did not wish to keep it, nor any of his possessions.

33

On the Friday my mother admitted him. My hopes that he might be changed for the better by his sojourn in Scotland were knocked when she came back down. She shook her head in sorrow and said the man was altered, and very much for the worse. From the damp wreaking air of Scotland, no doubt, and the poor diet they had, he was grown haggard and pale. And he was bedraggled in his appearance – but so too must anyone be after the long journey, she supposed. She herself would look like a scarecrow from all the shaking about, not to talk of the lack of sleep, for she knew what the beds in an inn were like. Maybe he had took to drinking the Scots whisky, she said, as he was like a man who was gone ragged from strong drink, so white he was and uneasy in himself.

'You are to go up to him, Sal,' she told me. 'There was nothing to be got out of him save that you are to go up.'

I did as I was obliged, with a heavy heart. He came forward, hands outstretched, to greet me. But I backed off and would not venture more than a step or two into the room. To tell the truth, he frightened me, not only on account of his state so thin and his sickly pallor that made the bones of his face stand out sharp as knives, but on account of the sense he gave off of an unnatural devotion and a craven need of me – and that before he had so much as uttered a word.

He came up and caught me to him and made to kiss me in our old way. But I turned my head from him. It was not that I would not. No, it was indeed that I could not. I was as much surprised and shaken myself by this reaction, I am sure, as he was.

'Tell me, Sarah, why you are grown so cold. Only tell me and I will put it right. I have gone so far for you, to Scotland and beyond. You cannot know how far I have gone. And will go farther, as far as you please, if there is a place that lies beyond that hell. Only tell me, Sarah, where I am to go.'

There could be no use, I saw, in my attempting to tell him my grievances, they were so many. His betrayal of me to Mr Patmore and that man's insolence, his presuming letters, and his putting me in the magazine for all the world to titter at. Words cannot be taken back. And if they could be wiped at a stroke, they are his nature and his occupation. And tomorrow or the next day he would offend me again even if he did not intend it, or know why it should offend me. My only defence was to give him no matter to tattle of.

Indeed, even if there was any use in talking, I was too choked up to make any sense. If my feelings were once comparable to the flame of a candle that is faint one minute and flares the next as the draughts take it, now they were the feeble red spark that remains when the candle is put out. Our relation was surely broken and there was no use in engaging in discussions, since it could not be repaired. I was fixed on silence.

'What has changed in you, Sarah? I beg you, let me know what I have done to displease you.'

'I am the same, sir,' was all I said.

He could not assert I had made promises to him. The

promises and protestations came all from him, like all the talk and all the fancies. Now he took refuge in making excuses for me.

'I am sure you are tired, Sarah,' he decided. 'We shall have a good talk tomorrow.'

He let me go. 'I shall sleep well at the least,' he declared, 'knowing that we two are under the same roof again.'

'I hope you shall always sleep well, sir, whatever roof you are under,' I answered.

He did not see what I intended by this, which was a farewell, as he did not wish to.

His breakfast-tray in the morning I left outside his door and had Betsy knock for him to take it in.

'What? Where is your sister?' he demanded.

'She is occupied with her work,' Betsy replied as I had bidden her.

He attempted a protest but she ran off before he could delay her.

All day I dodged him. He caught only a glimpse of me in the passage. And in the evening when I returned from the Roscoes I was glad to learn he was gone out. It grieves me to be unfriendly to anyone.

'I hope he has not taken to drink,' my mother exclaimed, 'for he will come in roaring and making trouble for us all if he has.'

Mother's principal fear concerning her lodging-house is that a gentleman will come in drunk and cause a rumpus.

I was resolved never to take Mr Hazlitt's breakfast to him again if I could help it, for then I would be drawn into the perils of intimacy and his tortuous converse. Shortly after Betsy had brought up his tray on the Sunday, Mr Patmore arrived. Mr Hazlitt called for another teacup and they breakfasted together. Then they went out.

My mother was obliged that day to go to Greenwich to see her sister who was ailing, and wished all of us to go too in case we should not see our relation again. But at the last minute Lizzie was obliged to go to Putney for a visit, for her nephew arrived in the cart to take her, and he could not be let go away disappointed when he had come such a distance. I dare say Mother was sorry enough to disappoint me but there was nothing to be done.

'Well, there is no help for it, you must stay, Sal, and keep the house,' she said. 'You shall have no bother, I'm sure, as all the gentlemen are gone out. We shall be home again near as soon as they are. In any case, do as you do, and be as you are, and you can come to no harm.' I need not say what she meant by that.

In the late afternoon I was irked to see Mr Hazlitt return, though without Mr Patmore. But his boy was with him, young Mr Hazlitt. Being alone in the house, though I was not inclined, I was obliged to carry up their tea. I was not fond of the boy, on account of his being rude to me before, but was glad of his presence now as a protection from his father's pleas and demands.

'Sarah, I am sorry if I ever said anything to vex you,' the young fellow said, coming forward when I had set down the tray and proffering me his hand.

'Then I'll think no more about it,' I agreed, and we shook on that.

I saw he was but a front for his father, who put him up to it, since it was what he himself wished to say and to have my pardon. He had not the courage to ask it for himself. Now he was assuming a breezy careless manner.

'I see you have brought me back my little Bonaparte,' Mr Hazlitt next remarked.

I was sorry he could think I might not return it. 'I told you I would keep him safe for you,' I exclaimed.

'But I gave him to you to keep,' he protested. 'I have

given you some little things before and he was one. But they were only tokens. In the future I will give you everything I possess, if you will only let me.'

I was astonished that he should break the rules which I believed had been laid down since his return, and ashamed that he should speak so bold in the presence of his son, who, though only a child, whatever his airs, had ears and an excellent understanding, and would have every right now to hate me. I left them before he could come out with any worse indiscretion.

In the evening when his son was gone, he called for his fire to be lit. This was but a pretext, because it was close as a day in August, and since he had only lately come from the bracing air of Scotland I am sure he could have borne the warmer air of London. Indeed, he had his windows open and never made to close them, but sat and watched as I blew the fire so that I feared his eyes might make holes like living sparks in my gown.

When it was scarcely lighting, he pulled me to my feet. As a rebuke I made to gain the door, but found that I dragged him after me and he was digging in his heels so I could make no advance. He drew up his chair and sat in it, clutching my wrist all the while.

'You see,' he said, 'I am seated as quiet and gracious as if we were in the parlour.' His voice trembled, belying the claim. 'You will not refuse to keep me company for a little while when we have been so long apart?' he pleaded.

It was said in the most soft and polite tone, but I had no choice of a refusal; I believe he would have kept me by force if I did. My hand grasped tight in his, he kept me talking for a good hour or more. It seemed like three.

He talked of his travels in the Highlands, and the ten pages a day he put up regular when he was living at the Renton Inn. That was a wild and windy place with a

Scots valley below for him to walk in. However, the beauty of it was all but ruined for him, he said, on account of my letters that he watched out every day for and they did not come. And those that did were a source of pain to him, since there was no word of affection in them. Well, it took me half the day to put down the few lines of business I did write to him. Despite all, however, he was able to be happy too, he said. 'For I was doing all that I could to assist my case with you, which is the getting of my freedom.'

I made no answer.

'It cannot serve me ill with you at least, eh, Sarah?' he pleaded.

There was a thing he never thought of – that there was nothing I could say that might serve *my* case with him that would not at the same time send him into a fit of temper and reproach. All I could hope for was that he might understand by my muteness my reluctance to hear him, and that then he might let me go.

He spoke of the lecture he gave in Glasgow. He gave it only for the fat fee that they were willing to pay, he said, for it was very hard to concentrate his mind on the works of Milton and Burns when it wished only to dwell on his Sarah and how she was faring so far away. As for his wife, I should be pleased to know that she was living up to her promise and proving as agreeable to his arrangements as a man could wish. From what he said, she was happy to go tramping about on her own in the Highlands while her husband was busy at divorcing her in the town.

'She never was a cantankerous or a complaining body,' he mused, 'though she is inclined to be greedy.' Here he grimaced. 'But that is an appetite that is easily fed,' he continued, cheering up, 'by the simple method of throwing guineas in her direction.

'There will be more than enough money for all,' he

declared, 'And more to come when I am happy and settled with my angel . . . My sweet consolatory girl,' he murmured, and played with my hair though I kept my profile cast down and away from him. 'What will I not be able to accomplish with my angel by my side?'

Still I remained silent, though the blood seemed to heat and curdle in my head like a pan of eggs, so vexed I was by his continuing so blinkered. Some of what he told me was of interest. But only because I could pretend to myself that it had nothing to do with me. There could be little harm in listening, I quieted myself, as long as I was not compromised by assenting to something I did not intend to carry out. I daresay I can be as commonsensical as Mrs Hazlitt, though I am not a vamp like she is, nor greedy either. It was only a matter of hearing him out and then he would be soothed and I could go.

I heard the others come in below from their outing to Greenwich.

'Where can Sarah be?' Mother asked Cajah.

'She is in Mr Hazlitt's room, I expect, like she always is,' Cajah answered. And my mother laughed and said something I could not make out. I am sure she must have said that it was in Mr Tompkins' room I had been more often to be found of late – for she well knew who pleased me and who didn't, though I never confided in her.

Mr Hazlitt, who was facing me, went down on one knee and began to plead his case with a pale and overwrought expression like an actor at Covent Garden. 'My love, you are like a queen, adorned with your own graces . . .'

I declare he must have fashioned himself after Macready. I could not endure it, to see him sentimental, and so comic, though it was the last thing he intended, when I could not return the play. If I were to join the charade he would be sure to mistake it for the reality. When all of a sudden he leaped up, I thought he had remarked my vexation. But he had not, instead he attempted to kiss me, and this time with an ardour that was not far from violence.

At this I succeeded in getting myself out of his grasp and ran from the room. I was resolved to never again kiss Mr Hazlitt, he had brought me such a deal of trouble. As I flew, I heard him follow quick down the stairs. But when I turned into the parlour and into mine and Betsy's room he came no further.

In a fury I threw myself on the bed. But before very long I was calmed by the knowledge that I had made good my escape and began to be sleepy, tired out as I was by Mr Hazlitt and his persistence. I wished Betsy would come up and tell me what they had discovered in Greenwich. Just then I heard a scream.

It was a horrid scream, of a character to wake a whole street, and it came from inside the house. Alarm at once rooted me to the bed. I was limp with terror and could not move. First I thought it was my mother and she was murdered, for the scream was high-pitched like a woman's. But it was so loud and strong and enraged that no woman could produce it, in particular if she were in an extremity of fear.

It was not repeated. But still I lay fixed to the bed as if stuck there with pins. It was a scream of anguish. But the blood-freezing quality in it came surely from anger, I reflected. My mother was not capable of such an excess of anger, nor was Cajah, nor certainly my father. In any case, what cause for such anger could they have?

Next I heard a great hurry on the stairs as everyone in the house rushed upwards past the parlour door, all shouting at once, 'He has her in his room, he has her in his room.' Divining before I did that the horror had come from Mr Hazlitt's chambers, they feared he was in the act of a ravishing or a murder. They were running to save me.

But there I was, alone and safe in my own room. Mr Hazlitt must therefore, I knew, have administered to himself a violence. They would find him lying in the middle of a red pulsing pond on the coloured rug. Or in a collapsed condition on the landing where he had fallen as he crawled in the direction of the parlour to find me, his life's blood flowing off in a cataract down the steps.

That was a prospect so vivid it was not to be endured. I buried my head in the bolster and screwed my eyes as tight as if the poor damaged fellow was stretched in his last convulsion on the boards by my bed. Rigid as the corpse itself was short to be, I waited for silence to fall on the house, the silence of the grave when it is all over for a person.

Still the shouting continued. And then I was persuaded that the self-murder or violence was still in train and he might yet be saved. Finding a morsel of courage, I crept to the door and listened in the gap.

I heard my mother cry out. 'Do not go out Mr Hazlitt. I beg you, sir, don't.'

By this I knew he was alive at least, and capable of walking – even, from the sound of it, of running. To have a madman rush headlong into the street and shriek slanders on the family frightened her, I dare say.

'Let him go. Let him go if he wishes it,' my father shouted.

The shouting was accompanied by a series of thuds and crashes on the stairs so you could think a carriage and four were galloping down. That was Mr Hazlitt taking the steps two or three at a time and all the rest of them in pursuit.

'What is up with you?' That was Mr Follett's voice, more clear and urgent than it was wont.

The shouts came closer now.

'What has she done to you?' That was Father's.

I saw I was no longer the cause for anxiety but was recognised as the source of his.

'She has murdered me,' he yelled, as clear and strong as in the play when the moment of truth is reached. 'She has murdered me. I am destroyed for ever. She has doomed my soul to perdition.'

Shortly after, a calm descended as if a gale had passed through the house but was now moved on. I could tell he was gone. There followed a hubbub as the matter was debated in low voices. Then that too died away. I could tell the lodgers had returned to their various apartments and the family to the kitchen. My strongest feeling by this time was gratitude that Henry was removed to Tooks Court and was not a party to the din.

'Where is Sarah? Is she safe?' I heard my father call.

Betsy's light step came running through the parlour and to our room. She looked in at me where I stood frozen behind the door, saw I lived, and ran off again, calling, 'She is here, she is safe.'

Shamed to show myself that night even to my family and worn out, I retired to huddle beneath the bed-covers. Betsy came back, with the smelling-bottle, that Mother sent up. I had but that for solace. Already I felt the injustice. Already I knew Mr Hazlitt could go about the town as he pleased, pouring insults on my head for the entertainment of his fine friends of character and principle, who might regret my cruelties to their heart's content and pity him sore for loving a tailor's daughter. I knew who had done the wrong, but there would be no gain to me in the knowledge.

An hour passed, maybe two, I could not say. Night fell. I was wretched and lit a candle to appease the dark.

Betsy reappeared. 'He has come back again,' she whispered.

'Mr Hazlitt? He is come back?'

'He ran off into the night. But a short while after was at the door again, asking to be let in. Father did not want to let him in but he insisted. Now they have gone up to his room together.'

I groaned and buried my face in the pillow. It was no longer a matter between him and me but one for the men to debate.

Betsy held up the candle to inspect me. 'Did he hurt you?'

'Words can hurt as bad as blows. Or worse, since they last, and if they are contemptuous enough can never be forgotten.'

'Mother says we must be careful of him as he has such a temper. He has smashed little Boney that you were keeping safe for him. The locket too. And the teapot with the birds and bees on it. They are all in bits on the rug. And the fire-irons are lying in corners where he flung them.'

I dare say he meant next to smash the window-pane and fling himself into the street, only he was stopped. It is a wonder he did not turn next to the fire he had obliged me to light and had not flung the coals too about the room, setting the house ablaze and sending us all leaping after him from the windows.

'Mother says we are to play him along,' continued Betsy. 'We are to behave as if nothing has happened, for that is the best way to quiet him. But you are to keep to your room and have nothing more to do with him.'

'I shall have no trouble in that,' I told her. 'If I were never to get up again I would be as happy.'

'I suppose he means to persuade Father to oblige you to marry him,' she said after a while.

'Father would not oblige me to do anything I do not wish.'

'Mother says she would not let you marry him even if you begged it. She declares she has no wish to see a daughter of hers turn black and blue from the violence he would offer you.'

'I do not believe he would offer me violence to make me black and blue. He would only strangle me with his love. But that would be no better.'

'But you should not be dull with him. He is a great man for causing excitements,' she suggested. 'To be dull might be worse.'

'To be made an angel and a queen is very dull, I can tell you, when you only know how to carry a slop-bucket and clean a grate and black a pair of boots.'

'But you are better than that, Sal,' protested Betsy. 'You can work flowers so neat and make out the meanings of books. Not many girls could make out Mr Hazlitt's books.'

'Well, he is not a divinity, though he thinks he is – so I cannot be an angel.'

'Do you wish me to go and listen at the door to what he is saying to Father?' she asked.

'No. He can tell him what he likes. It is all his own fancy anyway.'

With reluctance, for she is like Mr Hazlitt in that she loves a drama, Betsy gave up the idea and came to bed.

While she slept I attempted to summon the feelings of hate and contempt for him that he well deserved. But instead I could only weep tears for him and his despair and fell to wondering how I could make amends to him and restore his peace – short of marrying him. But since this was what he was fixed on, I could not see him agreeing to be content with anything less.

34

The next blow he struck should have had him up before the Assizes for treason. In the morning I discovered, from my mother's whisperings, that he was bent on betraying my honour and my privacy. He had told it all to Father – and cast in a more lurid light than I ever saw it or it deserved. How I was in his room hour upon hour – for he exaggerated the time I passed there – no, not polishing the grate or conversing or being instructed as my father expected, but lipping and fondling. These were the terms in which he represented our friendship and our endearments. My father was mortified by what he was told and shocked at the crude manner in which Mr Hazlitt expressed it.

'He said you let him enjoy you through your petticoats,' whispered Mother in my ear. 'I declare, I hardly know whether to laugh or cry.'

As it was hard indeed to make her cry and she did not laugh, I was well shamed. My father did not seek an interview with me on the subject. He was too grieved and vexed, Mother said, to be able to speak to me judicious. But he gave instructions that I was to stay out of Mr Hazlitt's way, that is unless I had a serious intention of considering his proposal. Otherwise our relation was likely to corrupt the pair of us. I dare say my father was more in sympathy with his admired Mr Hazlitt than he was with me. For men see women as little better than playthings or possessions who will be cold and treacherous if their owner is not firm with them. However, he was not of a mind to force me into anything, as I was yet, despite all, his daughter.

I had no wish, to say the least, in going near Mr Hazlitt as long as he persisted in playing the suitor. And my mother said she would as soon lose my company and my services by sending me off to her cousin's in Hounslow – with whom she had near as little acquaintance as I did, which was none – than put the house in danger of enduring another hey-go-mad. Greenwich was out of the reckoning as the story would surely kill my aunt, seeing her present frail condition. But I was to stay clear of him or she would be obliged to take some such action – if I were not sent to Hounslow I would be sent to Lizzie's sister's cottage in Putney.

Confined to my room and the parlour, I could not enjoy even the freedom of the stairs or the kitchen for fear that he would emerge of a sudden from his room or arrive home unexpected. It was particular gloomy and stifling to be shut in just then as it was the month of May when everyone else was going about again as free as birds. I was for all the world like a felon chained up in the dank air of Newgate.

Even had I permission to risk a stroll outdoors for some fresh air, I did not wish it, as my eyes were red and my nose pinched and shiny as a result of the tears I shed. I did not look well enough to go out. Why, I might run into Henry. I was as much afraid of meeting him in my teary state as I was of confronting Mr Hazlitt.

I hardly know who I cried for the most. Myself, shamed before Father and locked up. Henry, who I had a dear wish to see – though as long as I could still hope he would not hear of my shame, I must stay clear of him too. Or Mr Hazlitt, gone mad on my account, when he was once wise and happy and admirable in my eyes. Then the next minute I could weep for anger at him, and tell myself it was all his own fault that he was gone mad.

I could still feel for him the old tie of our affection. But I was above all frightened by him. I racked my brains for ways of calming him and jigging him out of his swoons and fanatics, that we might all be on our old and proper footing again. For the passion of another appears to us like a whim; you fancy he can be diverted from it, as you might distract a child's attention from a knife he wants for a toy by offering him a lump of sugar, and secreting the knife out of his sight in the drawer when he is not looking. But there was nothing in the world I could think of that might distract Mr Hazlitt.

Betsy took my place in attending him. As she is but a child she was safe, it was assumed, from his fits. A lover of excitements as she is, she was happy to trot up and down from his chamber to the kitchen and report the moods he was in and his conversations. She got as much amusement in that as Mr Hazlitt does in a box at Drury Lane. It is a useful talent to have in a lodging-house. I am sure she will be clever enough by and by, however, to advance above the position of the mistress of a lodging-house, though it is no bad thing to be. I could only fear I was marked for a great deal less.

35

A day or two into my captivity Betsy came running to our room with an ill-made little parcel. It was a present to me from Mr Hazlitt. On the screw of paper it was wrapped up in he had scrawled a message which at once angered me as it was written in the theatrical manner that I judge to be false. 'Pieces of a broken heart, to be kept in remembrance of the unhappy. Farewell.'

Inside the meagre screw I found the fragments of the little statue that he had hurled upon the floor in his fury though he had held it so dear. This, I thought, is how he chooses to treat what he claims to be an object of his esteem.

It grieved me to see Boney shattered. I left him, in pieces though he was, up safe on the dressing-chest. Betsy was vexed when I told her I had no answer to send, as she was deprived of her role as a go-between.

The following morning she came with a message no less offensive than the last. This was another parcel, more bulky than Boney's had been but no better wrapped. She brought too the news that she was requested to pack up his box. He was going out of town. 'But Mother says it could be a mood or a strategy and she will not believe it until she sees him and his box go down Chancery-lane.'

'Does he go back to the Highlands,' I asked, 'or someplace else? To Winterslow?'

She could not say.

The present he had sent was a set of three volumes, bound exceeding pretty in morocco. One of them was titled *The Man of Feeling*. This, I am sure, I was meant to take as a reprimand, for being insensible to his qualities of feeling, which were so superior to my own. I might have seen my way to accepting the books had he not committed the error of demanding in his note the return of the three volumes of his own hand that he had given me, in lieu.

This was a cut indeed. Excited as a colt waiting by the starting-post, Betsy stood by while I wrote my reply. I thanked him for the books, but said I had no need of them at present. And that he might have his own back but they would not be available until the afternoon as I had lent them to my sister and they would have to be fetched home. Back to him with the note went the *Man of Feeling* and his companions.

They were returned prompt to sit on the shelf in my room. For, on receiving my note, what did he do but offer them to Betsy, who did not know how to be ungracious and refuse them. She means in any case to be better read than I am before she has reached my years, so indeed she had no objection to their acceptance. But for the moment she likes only to stroke the bindings and admire the gilded letters.

I stole down the stairs to tell my mother that I had to go out to call on my sister and fetch home Mr Hazlitt's books. In truth, however, it was not Martha who had them but Henry. He had been curious some time previous about Mr Hazlitt's ideas, as they had a notoriety among the young men who were Henry's friends. But I do not believe that he ever read a great deal of them when I did lend him the works.

'Oh dearie me,' my mother said, 'I fear Mr Hazlitt is as jarred in his feelings as ever he was if he is asking for his books back. Next thing they will be landing on top of our heads as he flings them after us down the stairs.'

But she let me go when I said Betsy was to deliver them.

I was glad, you can be sure, to have a reason to leave my prison. But I arrived at Tooks Court all of a tremble from the fear that Mr Hazlitt's antics had come to Henry's attention, as well as information as to what had given rise to them. In that case, I thought, I would as soon never face Henry again.

Upon knocking at Number 6, the door was opened by a drab of a servant. 'I wish to see Mr Henry Tompkins,' I announced. Without any ceremony she directed me up the stairs to the first landing, which is not the practice in our house. A caller to a gentleman of ours is left on the steps – though in wet weather he may be invited to stand in the passage – until the gentleman permits us to say that he is at home and wishes to receive the visitor.

'Yes?' called out Henry's pleasing voice at my hesitant and nervous tap. When I entered, trembling as bad as ever, and saw the chamber he now lived in I thought that I must have a greater power over him than I knew. For to remove from our place to Tooks was surely a great comedown. His room was not half so fine as what he was used to with us. It had only a painted chest and the chintz coverlet was stained and patched and his small table listed in one leg. He was sitting bent over his law-books and at his elbow there lay a plate with the greasy end of a joint of beef on it that looked as if it was there yet from his dinner of the day before. Well, I could be happy at the least that he had no able servant, plain or pretty, who might take my place.

Any fears I could have had on that count were

proved groundless. For on looking up and seeing it was I who was come, he leapt to his feet and embraced me with his old frankness. Seeing him so handsome and weary and pleased, I thought I might as well die if I were to lose his esteem. But it is a harder thing to die than you might hope.

He kissed me, and wished for more than that too, I dare say. But the fear of Mr Hazlitt's temper and his running about the town saying who knows what was pressing on me. And I was afraid lest, Henry being so kind, my weeping would recommence and I might give myself away. I told him I would not stay as I was not quite well.

'Indeed, you do not look well,' he exclaimed. 'I do not like to see you suffer, Sarah. You are too frail. Would you care for some beef? I was keeping it for my dinner but you may have it.'

I declined, though indeed I should have liked to eat from his plate. But I could not touch a morsel, in particular since it was cold beef, and anyway he is frugal and might leave himself hungry if it were eaten. I was sorry to deceive him into believing I had the cold or the ache, but I dare say to suffer in the heart is no less of an ache than any other.

With a shrug at Mr Hazlitt's whims he turned up the books and gave them to me. 'Is Hazlitt off on his wanderings again?'

'I believe so.' I feigned to be vague.

Henry hoped I would soon be well again and I declared that it was not fair in me to keep him any longer from his studies. From the pressing manner of his kiss when I took my leave I knew he wished to detain me. But Mr Hazlitt with all his ranting had shown me the spectre of shame and robbed me of the freedom to kiss.

I went home with a heavy heart, thinking of Mr

Hazlitt lying there in wait for me, like a wild beast such as a tiger who is hardly tamed, and pondering why I could not turn him off – though I am sure no one but a fool could ponder long on that.

You could not say Mr Hazlitt was not solicitous. He, as much as Henry, could remark with a satisfactory anxiety on my frail and delicate health. But this was only because he wished to believe in it since it made me the opposite of his wife, who is a robust and healthy body.

If he wished me to be frail, frail I must be, though he did not mind to see me carrying a heavy pan of coal for his fire. If he wished me to be an angel, angel I must be, though I was streaked from the ashes. To Henry I was no more nor less than myself and that is as much as I ever wished to be.

36

Shut up in my room again, I cut my name out of the title pages of Mr Hazlitt's books where I had written it before. By this action I meant to signify that I did not intend any more to be always his friend and listener as I had fancied once I would, and that not so long ago. For to give a thing, and then to demand it back, is representative, I am sure, of a mean character such as one does not like to call a friend. To keep the memory of what you gave as a gift and see in it the purchase of a person or her affections is a low quality. There had been a time when I considered Mr Hazlitt a large and noble character.

I made up a tidy parcel of his books and put in with them each and every volume he had given me that was not of his authorship, among them the little crimson prayer-book with the green silk linings that Martha coveted so dear. She is more given to praying than I am. But if their lack meant I might be free of his advances I was glad to give them up.

On receipt of the parcel, he informed Betsy that she must carry the bulky object back to me again. 'I wish to retrieve from her only those volumes that I have written,' he protested.

'But, sir, they are the very ones she prizes the most,' she blurted out.

This was indeed the truth – though I would not be surprised if she said it out of mischief, she was enjoying to such a degree this novel form of a waltz, going back and forth with parcels and messages, and had no wish to stop.

At this he made another turnabout. He thrust the parcel into her arms and, seizing a twenty-shilling note from the table, thrust that in her bodice. Betsy was not of a mind to take it.

'You have made me happy again. It is a small price to pay for happiness,' he insisted. Now he set to discoursing and exclaiming about his happiness that was given back to him by her remark, and about the restoration of his love. All the while he paced about the room, his face as lit up as it had been dark before. The packing of his box that he had requested was of course suspended.

Bearing the selfsame parcel that she had left with, Betsy returned to me, and with her face downcast, despite the twenty shillings, as she well knew that by her remark she had made herself my gaoler. Here was Mr Hazlitt clutching his morsel of hope and turning it into a meal, and I confined even more strict to my room in consequence. He went out, bowing extravagant to the lodgers that he met on the stairs, though in general he had disdained to greet them, and murmuring and smiling to himself. Cajah saw him in the street and said he went along making curtesys before the horses and blowing kisses to the passengers, who grinned at him like he was a madman as they hurried on. However he was soon back again and asking for his tea to be sent up. Lest he be entertaining any hopes of seeing me, my mother went and told him that he must excuse me from my services any more as I was indisposed.

'Let her come at her own pleasure, ma'am,' he replied.

My mother would have liked to say that, in that case, he might be left to wait; but she was wary of inciting him into the production of another scene.

Several days passed in which his waiting continued. During that time Betsy reported that his patience appeared to be wearing thin, as he was growing sullen. And I skulked about the house like a thief, making a dash for the kitchen when I could not endure to be caged in my quarters any longer, or hiding in corners at the sound of a step.

At the end of a week he sent a note asking to see me. Fearing I could die of stagnation if this stalemate continued, or that he might throw another fit, I decided I must grant him an interview. My mother, by now weary of the business, was of the same opinion. I went, cool and businesslike, to him, the servant rather than the friend. He offered me his easy-chair and bowed in an elaborate manner when I agreed to take it. Then he knelt before me, which was a courtesy of his I had lost any capacity to endure. It signified I was in for protestations and theatricals. I stood, and made to leave.

'What have I done to you? Why do you hate me?' he demanded, blocking my path.

Only near-ruined me, I could have replied to the first. Made me a laughing-stock. Betrayed my confidences, regarded me as an object that has no will or independence of her own. Turned the house near upside down with your alarums . . . Is that not reason enough to hate? Excepting that I do not hate you in spite of all . . .

But I never could say to him what I wanted, more especially since he had no wish to hear it. All I could hope to do was to get away – and leave him by some manner with not a rag to pin his hopes on when I did.

'I always told you I had no affection for you.'

This cold lying statement pained me, near as bad as I believe it pained him to hear. It was hypocritical – and I consider a hypocrite the lowest type of person. But he had to be shocked into reason. With him, it was all or nothing. As he could not have me for his wife I must be less than the most distant of acquaintances.

As I might have expected, he would not accept the rebuff. He taxed me with citations of tender expressions that I had used on this occasion or that, when I had intended by them nothing more than the mildness of friendship. My anger rose.

'How could I ever have affection for you when you exposed me in front of the whole house and disgraced me?'

Oh, but indeed he was quite content with his conduct, since, according to him, I had brought it on myself.

'I own I have been guilty of improprieties,' I told him – and showed myself, I believe, to be better than he in being able to admit it. 'But in future I intend never again to be the subject of tittle-tattle but to keep the lodgers at a proper distance.'

Now he showed himself to be the hypocrite I had never thought him to be – and that might turn all his fine words to mockeries if a reader of his works had any sense. But no reader knows him as I do.

'It was all but to expose your honour to the world,' he protested.

He had to be always in the right. All his conduct and all his words are only to prove that he is right and we are wrong. If this is his motive are we right to think him wise?

'The purity of your character is like a rock to me amidst all the shifting treacherous sands of the world,' he continued rhapsodic. Again he sank to one knee. 'My love, my regard for you, amount to nothing less than adoration.'

'I have no use for adoration.'

He was only extravagant – this is how he termed his fits of temper – he said, when he doubted my perfection and had wished it to be demonstrated.

'Indeed, I am far from perfection, sir,' I protested.

He turned to the subject of the books which had travelled back and forth in Betsy's arms. How his heart had melted at her childish words as he realised that, despite all, he was dear to me. 'I felt as Adam must when Eve was created for him and she stood before him in all her compliance and all her radiance.'

At this I was sick at heart as much as vexed. He was fixed in his poetic notion of me as he was in all things and would not be brought to see reality where it did not suit him. If I ever was revealed as plain Sal to him and not a divinity he would have no esteem for me.

'I have heard enough of that kind of conversation,' I told him.

He questioned me as to whether I had any other attachment. I had half a mind to tell him that indeed I had.

'It will kill me to hear it,' he murmured and seized my hands so that he might not sink to his death unsupported.

I saw by this that he deserved no further confidences from me.

'Is it Mr Tompkins?' he asked, observing me keen as an alley-cat on the prowl.

I was frightened. Well, I could act as well as he. 'Mr Tompkins was here only a short time,' I replied with a careless toss of my head. I had a new fear now that he would challenge Henry to fight him in a duel. He would go and find him out as the cat finds the sparrow's nest. But of course Mr Hazlitt is too self-preserving for that, and would content himself with killing off my character and enlisting Mr Tompkins as his second. In the face of his questioning I had to gather every ounce of metal that was in me to prop up my light and careless manner.

'The divorce is in hand, Sarah,' he announced now, as if everything was understood and friendly between us and nothing had gone before. 'And you will marry me then.'

'I intend never to marry, as I am sure I have told you before. Only, you choose not to remember it,' I said with a laugh.

By this I hoped to console him with the knowledge that if I would not have him, at least I would have no other man either for my husband. But it only sent him into a fury. His countenance was dark and swollen like a lowering sky that cannot make up its mind where to drop its freight of din and destruction. Patches of livid white stood out on his high forehead and cheeks. He had the terrible look of imminent death. Only his eyes showed life – and they shone dull with an unnatural depth like Betsy's velvet tippet the night it took fire from the candle. The bones in his face were working so you could expect that any minute they must grind and break under the pressure of his feelings.

All of this gave him such a terrible mixed expression of anguish and contempt and cravenness that I was filled with alarm for him. I had to rein myself in from taking his poor hurt head to my heart to soothe it. For, assuage him as that might for a day or a week, it could do him no favour, for it would only drop him into a chasm of hope and prolong his agony. For his sake I had to stand firm. Then he might learn to hate and despise me. Then, I believed, he would short enough forget me.

And Henry might be saved from despising me. And

my character, though it was cracked like an old teacup, might stay in one piece and still be serviceable.

He found words at last. They came out at full gallop, like a horse-regiment charging into battle. 'Your only wish, though it is very fervent, is to murder me. You are tearing my heart from its place. You would stab me in my very soul, though I love your soul better than my own. You are sister to the serpent who wraps her lecherous coils around a man and pretends it is a fond embrace. You are poisoning me, your soft lips are fangs that sink into mine and deposit their foul juice . . . You are seed of the serpent who brought doom and despair on all men . . . And yet' – here he shook his head from side to side as if to rid it of a frightful vision, and his features broke up into a painful smile – 'you are clothed in the raiment of a beauteous angel and, Sarah, I do not care. I cannot give you up and though you may be the demoness herself or her woeful child, I love you – and you may hate me as you will if you will only have me.'

He stretched out his arms to me.

Already I was backing away and was on the stairs. He followed and threw himself on the boards, his head thrust between the rails. He uttered loud moans. I was on a level with his livid working face and his white knuckles where they clutched the posts. My legs turned weak and refused to move.

'Forgive me, only say you forgive me, or I shall die. Oh, let me die this minute. For what is my life to be without you? No, you will forgive me, I cannot die while you yet live . . .'

The power to move returned to me and I ran down the flights of stairs, his pleas assaulting my ears, and ran into the garden and hid behind the wall of the small-house until I could not hear them any more.

I never did believe any man could die for love, they have too much else to occupy them. They say such things only to appear in a noble light. Still, I was unwilling to go in for fear of what dreadful sight might face me. When at last, lacking my shawl and starved with cold, I was obliged to go in, I found him living and his colour even restored a little. He was sitting peaceful as a lamb in Father's place by the fire in the kitchen and my mother opposite, for all the world like an uncle with whom you need have nothing to do but be carefree and pretty so he might regard you with fond smiles.

They had been talking of me, I could see, my mother having taken on the task of pacifying him the way I would have liked to – but at a remove, so there was little danger in it.

'You see,' he remarked, with the calm, kind tone of an uncle come in from Hampstead or some country village to see us, 'Sarah does not look as if she hates me. Do you not say so, Mrs Walker?'

I believed he was resigned now to the knowledge that this was as much as he could ask for. My mother, as calm as Mr Hazlitt, agreed that indeed I gave no impression of hating. He wore the mild sad smile aged people wear sometimes when they regard a younger. I left them, lest his tone should alter. I knew the strength of his mind could vanish as fast as a heap of snow under a shaft of sunlight.

On the following day, he left us without any further ado, and returned to Scotland.

37

I was able to breathe easy again and give up lurking in corners like a pickpocket from Seven Dials, and go about the town as I pleased, and talk to whosoever I liked. June was come in with its breezy and joyous balm and I could take the air and hope to meet Henry. My sister warned me that I should not call on him at his lodgings or I would be compromised, no matter how ladylike my conduct. I could tell she thought the worst of me. My mother too advised me the same, at Martha's bidding, I am sure. I contrived, therefore to meet him in Chancery-lane as he was turning into Lincoln's Inns.

At sight of me he doffed his hat and smiled most gay and tender. 'Sarah,' he exclaimed, 'I have missed you sore this past week.'

I saw that no word of the scandal to do with Mr Hazlitt and myself had come to his attention. He placed my arm in his and we went along at a slow pace. I was flurried and made nervous by being so proximate to him, so I was unable to talk or be gay, and the press of passengers was so great that there was hardly room for a foot's pace. He too seemed disinclined to talk and after some time walking up and down in a kind of delighted misery he murmured that we might repair to his room and be out of the throng. I was sure he too longed to taste a kiss that was so long postponed.

I had made no promises on that score to Martha nor to Mother but had heard them out in silence. All the same I took my time in assenting to the proposal.

'I want only a kiss, Sarah,' he murmured. 'You are persuaded, I hope, that I would never harm you.'

We were scarcely in his room before he caught me to him so hard that my feet left the boards and he kissed me so passionate that my breath near failed. His complexion was grown pale and damp, as if all the blood had left it – and I knew very well where it was gone. Only his eyelids closed over his eyes were flushed. But it was nothing like the whiteness near to lime that Mr Hazlitt showed so often in his face and had nothing in it, you can be sure, to frighten me.

I confess he might have had me then without a pang if he tried – in spite of the way they would have you think a girl has not red blood coursing through her, but some pale calculating fluid, and indeed that this is admirable stuff to have in her veins. But here I was put down and placed at arm's length and Henry flung himself aside on to the bed.

'I shall not ruin you, Sarah,' he groaned. 'But, I declare, I should marry you this day if I could.'

I wished to embrace him but he pushed me away.

'You are a dear, innocent girl,' he said. 'You do not know what things a man is capable of.'

I kept my gaze cast down for fear he would see me flush up.

'You possess the sweetest profile of any girl I ever saw,' he murmured. 'If my father could know it, and know what an excellent girl you are, he would be convinced of the strength and rightness of my feelings and he could have no objection to you.'

Here was my old fear returned. I felt an ache as of my

heart sinking, when it had been so full, and my mouth trembled.

'He objects to me because I am the daughter of a lodging-house,' I observed after a little when he remained silent. 'He tells you, I am sure, that you may as well marry a serving-girl. But if you were to do that, he would cut you off.'

'But you have not the face of a serving-girl. Nor the mind of one. No, indeed you have not . . . Do I offend you, Sarah?' He was anxious at once.

'It is only what the world thinks.'

'Not the world,' he protested. 'Only my father, who is an elderly rustic gentleman and fancies a plain vicarage spinster who says her prayers will make a better wife than the prettiest girl in London, whose pleasure it is to read the works of the eminent Mr Hazlitt.'

At this my heart seemed for an entire minute to cease its beat. But he remarked nothing, only lay back on the coarse grey pillow.

'The vicarage girl, of course, will have at least a hundred a year.'

I was not surprised to hear that and was only glad that he had departed from the subject of Mr Hazlitt.

When I bent to pick up my shawl from where it had fallen, he jumped up and arranged it about my shoulders as he liked to see it.

'Let us give up this heavy theme,' he said, 'and be gay. We will go out and take a cup of chocolate in the Southampton Coffee House. When I am with the girl I like best in the world I am entitled to be gay.'

And soon we were laughing and happy as ever we were. More so, indeed, as the talk had brought about an advance in our understanding and we saw plain how things stood between the two of us – of which the most important was that we were uncommon fond of each other.

38

Quitting my presence did poor Mr Hazlitt no good by all accounts. Indeed, it appeared to have made him worse. Word of his doings came all the way from Scotland, to Mr Roscoe and Cajah, and anyone else who cared to listen, repeated by the gossips who hang around Mr Patmore.

He was wandering around the streets of Edinburgh in as rampaging and wild a manner as the gales that blow incessant there. He would not keep his room nor settle to a conversation with the friends who took an interest in him, but would go off muttering nonsense to himself. He had alarmed more than one man who was not even in the company, by clutching him by his neckcloth in a strangling way, and informing him how very hurt he was in his mind. He was gaunt as a hungry wolf – though he was gaunt enough before – and his hair was turned white so you could hardly know him, and his dress more unkempt and unseemly than ever it was.

It grieved me to think of him in so bad a state. And I grieved for myself more, as I feared his madness might induce him to speak of me and lay on me the blame for his hurt. But I did not yet consider him to be capable of such treachery and no-gentleman conduct as that. I was consoled in any case when I remembered that no one in

Scotland knew anything of me who was far away in London – and they had enough maids there that they did well know, to gossip of.

I was in receipt of a parcel from him towards the end of the month. My spirits soared when I saw what it contained – a red and shining length of tartan silk. But they dropped again just as quick.

'It will make a splendid gown,' exclaimed Mother, seizing it from me. She cast the silk before us as she does the linen sheets to be folded, and it rippled crimson in the gloom, lending our dull familiar parlour the gleam and adventure of the foyer in Covent Garden. But it would never be made up. Seeing where it came from, I could never wear it and be honest.

'There would be no good in having it made up,' I told my mother. 'It is too bright a shade for a girl of my station to go about in.'

'It would suit your colouring,' she protested, for she did not like to see such a nice length of silk waste away in a drawer.

Still I put it away.

The letter that came in the parcel was sober written. It had nothing in it to offend me and was quite lacking in endearments. But I liked it no better than any other I had received from him, as it displayed his despair and therefore his persisting excess of feeling just as the others displayed his foolish optimism.

He asked in it that I forget the past and agree to 'judge me by my conduct in the future'. Well, I judged that this control which he now professed in his style was but a fragile thing and would be sure to collapse at the hint of a wrong word or look from me. As a postscript he wrote, 'You may be pleased to make up the silk tartan for a gown to wear to the play when you go there with your lover.' I did not believe for a minute in this pretence at renunciation.

I could see no way of replying. But I left the letter lying about for them all to study as they wished. By it, they would be assured I had done nothing wrong.

Martha pressed me more than once to let her know my feelings for Mr Hazlitt. 'Could you never consider taking him as your husband?' she asked with a feigned disinterest.

'I do not wish to speak of my feelings in that regard.'

'Why, Sally? Can you not speak to your sister?'

'They are my own. And to speak of them only gets me into trouble.'

'Never with me,' she protested.

What a decoy is my sister. If I did tell her any of my secrets, such as my going to visit Henry in his lodging-house, she would lament as if I had done a murder.

'Would you say that he repels you?' She was talking of Mr Hazlitt.

'No,' I said at last, believing there could be no harm in admitting to that.

'You have some tender feelings towards him then?'

'I have some such,' I conceded.

She put down her work and examined my expression. 'He is divorcing his wife for your sake, Sarah. You should speak plainly to him.'

'The divorce is all for his own sake. I have tried to speak plain to him but he does not listen to what I say. It is all his fancy, if he says I made promises to him.'

'There is no necessity, Sarah, to shriek like a fishwife.' She was near as warm as I was by this time.

'I am sorry for shrieking,' I said. 'But let us not speak any more of it.'

'I am no more wise as to what you wish, or what you intend,' she sighed.

I made to flounce off and she was obliged to give up the subject.

It was not she who wished in particular to know my

intentions but her husband. And he was interested in them only to pass them on to Mr Patmore – who would in turn pass the information on to the person in question. A woman when she is married gives her loyalty to her husband and would betray her sister, though she once shared a bed with her too, and for longer indeed. That is reason enough to despise marriage – though I dare say I would do the same for Henry and he is not even my husband. You can despise your own actions and yet carry on doing them.

I was made conscious that Bill Hazlitt's afflicted mind and the reason for it were the talk of London – the part of London that Mr Patmore frequented, at any rate. And that was the part that affected me, as I had my own place in it, small though it was. The state of my mind on the other hand took no attention, as they would not bother to consider the feelings of a tailor's daughter. In any case I gave them no cause for amusement in watching my theatrics, as I would die rather than expose my feelings as Mr Hazlitt did, but kept them locked away. This is a girl's only defence. She must be impassive and stony as a statue if she does not want to be mocked and taken advantage of.

At night I would lie awake, suffocated by the stale and heavy air and the fear that the sorry tale would come to Henry's ears. I hoped most ardent he would not be told it. But time and again I wondered whether I should not be the first to relate it to him, if he had to know of it. How Mr Hazlitt had grown a passion for me, but only out of his love for being dramatic and his desire for notoriety. Why, to make me the subject of gossip proved he did not love me. I was only an object for his passion, which was ready just then to burst out when he came to live with us – and I had the misfortune to be convenient when he was obliged to expend it . . .

But if I did, Henry could think me light, a girl who dallied with men for the sake of inciting them. If Mr Hazlitt could cause me to doubt myself and my actions, well, Henry too might doubt them. As a man, he might be obliged to ally himself on the side of Mr Hazlitt. After all, at the least hint of lightness in her, a woman, though he once cared for her, is as foreign and contemptible to a man as is a Portuguese.

I hoped I was as open and artless with Henry as a girl could be. But to be closed and artful is the only way for a girl to preserve herself and her reputation. You cannot succeed at both. And they are ready to accuse us on any grounds. We are expected to be constant when they are not. Why, it would not surprise me to espy Henry with a common woman of the town just as I have espied Mr Hazlitt. They expect us to know what we want but never to ask for it. They expect us to be hot and yet to shrink back as if we do not know what heat is. To have the wit of admiring their minds but not have a contrary word to give back. To be modest in our dress and yet calculate display. To care nothing for tin and yet arrange it so that our children will rise in the world . . .

Oh, I am low in spirits and angry as a girl should never be. Yet I could not choose to be a man, despite all their advantages, since I wish to be kissed by one – or two, if I like. Though this is a pleasure I should not taste for the trouble it brings. Well, they have taken everything from me excepting my freedom to think as I do. A girl can be stopped from anything, excepting thinking.

I might have done myself a service by telling Henry. I might have made a case for myself.

Mr Patmore called to see us. You could think us as friendly with him as he was with Mr Hazlitt. It was only of course to relate the fruits of his spying to his friend. And he had no objection to doing the thing in reverse.

Mr Hazlitt, he told my mother – and she appeared to be as glad as he to hear it, though my spirits fell into a sink – was just now divorced, or would be within the week, please the lawyers.

'Well, there's a fine thing,' exclaimed Mother. 'He has gone and done it, as he said he would.'

The long wait for it, went on Mr Patmore, had put the poor fellow into an excitable frame of mind, of which a consequence was that he had come to doubt his welcome when he returned to us. Mother said lawdy, there was nothing new in that. He had been in an excitable frame of mind before ever he went to Scotland, for months past indeed. And it was up to his friends to quiet him as best they could.

'You have no objection to having him back?' asked Mr Patmore, all the while examining me in his meaning way.

'This is his home and we are his friends, I hope,' my mother said. 'If he is in want of an asylum, he shall always have it here. We would never turn away a gentleman such as Mr Hazlitt.'

And off she went on her chant of how Mr Hazlitt could be indeed as much of a handful in the house as a brace of children when he let himself be riled by some trifle – 'But my husband says this comes from the brilliance of his mind and there is nothing to be done but to treat him with the kindness and courtesy that such a man deserves.'

And Mr Patmore nodded away approving, while he watched me all the while for some hopeful reaction or sign of affection that he could convey to Mr Hazlitt. Here I left them, for I knew from the exchange that my mother was wobbly as a jelly and would be no assistance to me in the situation I found myself in with Mr Hazlitt. Oh, she may doze through the play, but she loves excitements and intrigues on her own stage and is more than ready to play her part in them. I saw she was no better than Mr Patmore, who was going between our place and the Roscoes' in Dyer's Court, and writing down all that he learned or fancied to send on to Mr Hazlitt, while I was nothing more than a doll to be dangled between the lot of them.

I was coming to fear now that Mr Hazlitt was revered as such a genius that my family began to be of a mind to throw me to him for a sacrifice, as a Christian used be thrown to a hungry lion. And I was myself indeed beginning to feel so tired and powerless to withstand him that there were times when I thought I may as well walk peaceable into his cage to be eaten, and make an end of it. Then I would remember Henry and my courage returned.

Soon another letter came from Edinburgh. I saw Mr Patmore had done his work. The tone of it was tender and hopeful and seemed no less dangerous and no more answerable than those that had come before.

'I long to see your sweet face . . . I promise that I shall never again be angry with you, my dear little statue that has her niche always in my poor heart . . .'

Yes, as long as you will be mine, inside wedlock or out of it – he had sense enough not to say that.

This letter went the way of all the rest.

'They say Aul' Reekie could not come up with a match for our Sal,' crowed Cajah. 'Are you to have him after all? Better a dotie than a fool, eh, Sal? Which shall you take? Your elderly genius or your young dimwit of a lawyer?'

If only Mr Hazlitt had met a lass with a ginger frizz to take his fancy in Auld Reekie. He would not have troubled then to show me up as a jilt and a whore. I never thought a few kisses and endearments, that were little more than you might bestow on a child, could bring that doom on a girl. Now, Henry may have better reason in truth to lay such charges at me. Oh, when he felt me under my petticoats I hoped indeed he would throw me to the floor and pull them up over my head. I do not believe Martha can have felt half as much for Mr Roscoe or she could not be calm and careful as she is. I dare say I was always more capable of ruin than she was.

However, I would not consent to visit Henry in his apartment any more. I am capable of ruin but I am also capable of resolve. I told him it was too sultry and airless to sit in – though in July the Park itself is near as close and damp as the kitchen is on washday. He made only a little protest and walked along sedate beside me. But when the crowd was scarce about us he took the opportunity to put his arms tight around me. Our conversation was inclined to be stiff, lacking the lightening influence of a kiss. However, I think he grew no less fond of me in consequence, nor I of him. I own my sister may after all have the right of it, with her little lady principles.

39

Towards the end of the month Mr Hazlitt made his reappearance. He was further changed, along the pattern he had set when last we saw him. If I had hoped for any alteration in his feelings, however, I would have been disappointed. Indeed, it was the absence of any such alteration that wrought the change in his person and made it all the more distressful. The black hair quite gone, the face etched with lines, his clothes hanging loose. He was grown old. But he was no more wise.

I greeted him when we met on the stairs, and gave him my hand, for I could do no less. He reached out to me, all a tremble and with such a mangled look of suffering and hope that I was unable to meet it and turned my head away. We exchanged a few common-place and polite words about his journey from Scotland. He told me he had travelled on a smack and been very ill. 'Very ill, Sarah,' he repeated and with great significance. I assured him he would be better by and by, and when he said he would like his tea sent up I took the opportunity to withdraw.

I set out the tray but my mother mounted with it, since I refused, and grumbled as she went. She seemed to have discarded her old rule for me, that I should keep out of his sight. He kept her above for a long time.

She came down shaking her head in wonder but with an appearance of amusement as well. And wanted no prod to recount the extravagant proposals he had made to her. He desired to take the whole house, or at least all the lodgings in it, at a rent of a hundred pounds for the year.

'He thought Sarah looked so tired and pale. And since she would in consequence have only himself to look after, she would have little work to do and might enjoy some repose, and go strolling abroad in the fresh air as she pleased . . . Where would Mr Hazlitt find a hundred pounds?' she laughed. 'Mercy, he owes near twenty pounds to your father.'

There was a general laugh. I was glad to see by it that the others were no less eager than I was to know she would not hear of entertaining that proposition. Apart from a want of faith in his ability to pay, what is the use of a lodging-house without lodgers and the company and occupation they provide? I am not so fond of stitching and of walking that I would want to do nothing else – and I was sure Mr Hazlitt would not be happy to pay for my walks with Henry. My mother likes to be buried up to her elbows in a basin and to be ordering us about to do this chore and that. She was not made to be a lady and to be owned by a gentleman, and her daughters with her. 'If he had his way,' she said, 'we would all be at his beck and call and starve into the bargain.'

But she had kept the more curious proposal for last, to be better savoured.

'Fancy, I have been invited to travel as far as Scotland,' she announced then, laughing all the more. 'Mr Hazlitt wishes me to accompany the pair of you, Sarah, if you are to be married. I am to go along as your chaperone.'

'I shall not go,' I said, near faint that it had gone so far.

'You must if you accept him, since it was there he got his divorce. But indeed I hope you do not intend to accept him, as I have no wish to go anywhere, let alone to Scotland.'

She had said the same about the play, but had been easy persuaded in the end.

I did not feel quite safe after this. I feared they were all plotting behind my back for the sake of peace. And before I knew it, I might find myself clutched between him and Mother in the coach, racketing along on the road to the north, and dressed up in a wedding-gown.

For the present, due to Mr Hazlitt living again in the house, I was returned to my confinement – though now it all was my own decision, as Mother gave an impression of having washed her hands of the situation. He was like a ghost who haunted the stairs, waylaying me to fetch him some article and delaying me with his pleading and meaning looks. I was as helpful as I should be, but cold – as it would have well served me to be from the start.

I had not seen Henry for some time. A week seemed long to me when I did not see him. At the end of such a week, I was sitting in the parlour by the window, mending a shirt of Father's, for my mother would not brook me working pink petals when there was mending to be done. I had insisted on sitting there as I had a rash hope that he would pass and I could call down to him. Might we take a turn as far as Exeter Change? Seeing as he had talked of wishing to visit Chunee the elephant and the other beasts in the menagerie . . . And then I remembered the great peril it would be to be about on the thoroughfares with Henry as there was a chance of running into Mr Hazlitt. I became quite melancholy at the thought of my constrained position. At the end of it all, it was only Mr Hazlitt who tracked me down.

He put his head in the parlour door with the businesslike friendliness that I perceived to be false. It was an air which attempted to give the impression that he was favouring me with a little converse when in truth he had better things to do elsewhere and would soon be off. In reality he was but judging the strength of my hostility.

'May I come in?'

'If you wish.'

He sat close by me on the window-seat and took my hands so I was obliged to put down my work. To refuse him them would only incite him to argument.

'Ah,' he said, observing that I was occupied with a shirt, 'I have some shirts you might care to work. I wish to have some frills put on. Would you care to do that for me, Sarah?'

'With pleasure, sir,' I said. And meant it most sincere, if that was all he would ask of me.

'What have you done with the little image, Sarah?' he asked then.

'It is broken. But the fragments are safe, sir, on top of my dressing-chest.'

'Might it be mended?'

'It is in several pieces,' I said doubtful. 'And the little sword is gone. It can never be as it was.'

'Could you try, Sarah, and see if it might be patched together at least?'

I agreed that I would try, and took up my stitching again with a silent plea that he should let me be. But no, that was too much to expect. He took the needle and cloth from my hands, though gentle enough, and coiled his fingers about mine and stroked my palm.

'I sent you a fine piece of plaid silk from Edinburgh, Sarah, did I not? Have you not had it made up? Would it not make a pretty summer gown? I have hoped to see you wear it.'

'But the summer will soon be over,' I objected. 'By the time it is made up it will be cool enough for worsted. It must wait for next summer, sir.'

'Next summer,' he murmured, his gaze bent on me with a look of hope I could not endure. 'Shall I see you in the tartan next summer, Sarah?'

At the knowledge that there was no comfort I could offer him, and none surely for me either, tears started into my eyes. So that he might not remark them I bent over my work, though I was stitching blind, for my eyes were clenched shut for fear of drops falling.

'Next summer shall not be sad and confused like this one, eh, Sarah? It shall be like the last when we were friends and you came bounding into my room in your delight at seeing me.' He pressed his forehead to mine. It was bony and damp and foreign to me. 'Oh my sweet Sarah,' he groaned, 'tell me we shall be once again as we were then.'

There was nothing I could say to grant him hope. And yet nothing to pain him either, any more than had pained him already. He at least had the release of speaking. My tongue had a seal on it, like solid wax. That prison, the prison of silence, is as bad as any one made of stone.

No longer able to keep the press of tears from dropping, I jumped up. If I were to give up my reserve and weep in his arms, the pair of us would be lost and I no less wretched than he. He took a step towards me and I moved back from his reach. I was obliged to take out my handkerchief from my pocket to stem the flow.

'How beautiful you look,' he exclaimed with a coolness that exasperated me. 'Your expression is so heavenly that I am incapable of believing . . .'

My expression, I am sure, was a begging one that he should leave me in peace.

'All this time that I have been absent from your presence I have longed to see that look once more. I believed I could die happy if I did. But I was wrong. I cannot be separated from it unless it should pass with me into the shades.'

I had feared he might kill himself on account of me. The house feared it also and intended to keep him from it by all reasonable means. Now I saw he might be of a mind to kill me too.

It was he who had come to disturb me, but now it was I who left him in possession of the parlour, on the instant.

I still had the idea that it might be possible to restore the relation between us to a manageable one by a proper and seemly playing at the servant. He left down three of his shirts to me, and I frilled them and sent them back with Betsy, together with a message that I should be glad to frill as many more as he wanted. I wrapped up Boney's smashed pieces and carried them to three different places until I found a man in Somers Town who agreed he might make some job of putting him together. I fetched him packages of his Bohea from Twining's as I always had – though he was not taking so much of it now. After all, he was writing but little. Also, Mr Roscoe told us he had reverted to his former habit of ale-drinking.

But he could not have been a great deal in the taverns for he prowled about the house on the slightest pretext. I watched out for him and kept out of his way so he scarcely saw my face. When he went out he could stop in the street for half an hour continuous, gazing up at the parlour window as if willing me to appear at it.

'She is going out more than she was used to,' he remarked to Betsy, with a keen look.

'I do not think so,' Betsy replied. 'Should she not, sir?'

'Where does she go when she goes out?'

'Just now she is gone to fetch some eggs for a plum cake.'

'In what direction is the shop where she fetches the eggs?'

I believe he would have followed me if he could. But I am slight and nondescript and easy to lose among the passengers in the streets. Maybe that is why he wished me to go about in his red Edinburgh plaid, so he could keep a better eye on my movements. I declare he would have liked me to be prominent as easy game, like the red deer they stalk with guns in the Highlands of Scotland.

But all this harassment was only a trifle and a nuisance in comparison with what he did next. I thought it at the time very hard to bear − but indeed had I known the worse that was to come I would have been more than content to put up with it.

40

The little image was mended and I decided to return it to him myself, since it meant such a great deal to him, and once had meant not a little to me too. But when I entered his room, and presented it with a smile that I judged to be neither warm nor cold, he hardly looked at it, nor did he even care to inspect the new pieces the man was obliged to make up, and had put in all so neat. Setting it aside as if it were no more outside the regular than his packet of tea, he sank to his knees in his imitation of Mr Macready. Seizing my hands, he plastered them with kisses. I dare say that was indeed an error, not to have kept firm and sent Boney up with Betsy.

'That these hands might be as they once were. Loving, tender hands. That is all I ask,' he exclaimed.

I was made so weary by him and so resigned to his excesses by now that I had not the strength to wrest them from him.

'Pity me,' he cried. 'Pity me – and save me if you can.'

But my pity too was near worn-out. I felt I should not look on his face again. It would not be just if I did, since I could not look on it with the degree of kindness he was seeking. With a final hope that he might comprehend me, I gave him a look to signify my last farewell and withdrew.

Fearing I would suffocate in the house with such a figure of pathos awandering in it, I went out. I suppose if ever a girl was in need of a true friend, then I was. I had none. Henry was indeed my friend, but if I did not take care he could cease to be – and so he was the last I should pour out my heart to. All the same my steps, wanting in commonsense of their own, led me in the direction of Tooks Court. By chance, he was on the doorstep.

'I was considering going to fetch you, Sarah, for a stroll,' he called out. 'And here you are, come of your own accord.'

It was consoling indeed to place my arm in his. But I was constrained in my mind and heart and holding myself careful, like when you carry a jug that is brimming, for fear it may spill. He had on a new pair of yellow gloves that he was rather fond of. I admired them but perhaps not with the gaiety he was used to. He remarked I was quiet.

'You are often quiet. But today you are excessively quiet. Is there something on your mind that worries you?'

I replied that there was nothing. I feared that if I commenced to tell, I would reveal too much or he could surmise it. Then the jug would fall to the ground and it would all seep out and he would break with me for ever. We went along in silence.

'Maybe I tire you, Sarah, with walking?' he suggested.

I longed to fling myself in his arms and press myself to him and smother my swollen heart in his. But if I did, the jug would shatter with a fearsome crash on the cobbles. 'A little. But I am in need of exercise and have no objection to going on,' I replied with an attempt at gaiety.

We had not gone very far when he suggested that we turn about, saying he would accompany me as far as the Inns. He showed no desire to talk any more. I began to fear he found me tedious or to think I was no further use to him.

Now we were in King Street. A parade of folk was strolling forward and back and others holding up their passage as they stopped to chatter, or to inspect some jumble in a shop window. I began to find it difficult to breathe, what with the dust they were setting up, and wished ardent that there were not so many persons about us. I longed for a wide and empty road to walk on, my arm in Henry's, with tall chestnuts hung over it for a cooling shade and a light zephyr rustling the leaves and giving a stir of air, and the houses set well back from the thoroughfare to provide a prospect. Well, I should not give up the houses. I should be lonely if there were no houses. But they should be new-built of yellow brick and elegant.

Glancing up for a change, to compare, I dare say, those fancied houses with the crooked constructions of smoke-stained and grimy brick pressing in about us, my eye glimpsed a familiar figure. I could not mistake it, not with that stare, brooding yet fierce, and alert to all the wrongs that had been done to him. Here was Mr Hazlitt, bearing down upon us. He was come out in search of me, I could tell, his coat askew and without his neckcloth. My heart near stopped.

Still I went on. If I were his wife itself, I'm sure I would be entitled to take a turn in the public street. And with whosoever I elected for my companion. All the same, I would have turned and fled like a common thief who has just tugged a pearly ring from a lady's little white finger if it meant I might escape him. But already his stare accused me so you could think I were none other indeed than that same contemptible felon, or worse.

My feet carried me onwards. I had not the will to lower my gaze, though I am sure it was blank as a marble statue's not full hewn. I saw his tormented look travel from me to my companion. We went on.

Henry squeezed my arm. 'Was that not Mr Hazlitt we passed just now? I declare, I would hardly know him. He is become such an aged and troubled-looking fellow. And he did not deign to greet us, though he looked us over hard enough. He might at least have greeted you. Does he not live with you yet, Sarah?'

I murmured an assent. We reached the end of the street.

'Let us turn,' he said. 'I shall take you home. You are uncommonly pale.'

I wished dear to go on. I wished never to turn, but to put an impassable distance between me and my tormentor. I found my voice.

'Am I not often pale? You have said so before.' I attempted gaiety.

'Yes, but just now you are pale as a little phantom who might fade away from my sight at any moment.'

'That is but the heat. It has not let up all day.'

'Well, I should not like you to fade away, whatever the cause.'

He turned, obliging me to follow, and we retraced our steps that had been so painful. We passed the inn called the Mouse and Cat. There was a break just then in the phalanx of passengers. And Mr Hazlitt loomed up dark before us once more.

I was no more composed than I was before, though now my heart beat fast as a crazy clock, giving me to hope that I might pass away as a consequence. At least then they might take pity on me.

I met his eye. I thought he intended to obstruct our

path. But no, he stood aside to let us pass. We went on. I waited, my breath stopped once more, on a shriek fit to wake the dead at our backs, such as he let loose before when he was crossed. None came.

'Well, he is a strange fellow and no mistake,' murmured Henry.

I was sure he had felt the same expectancy, though he could have no reason to.

'Again he gave you no greeting, Sarah, but gazed stricken at you as if you are indeed a phantom.'

And now it was he who looked at me so hard that he walked straight into a coster's cart of cold pasties. The little incident distracted him and gave me a moment to compose myself. 'Did you injure yourself?' I was able to ask, for he was rubbing his shin, and I was glad, you can be sure, of a change of topic. He winced on coming upright but assured me the hurt was nothing.

'Mr Hazlitt is not well at present,' I mustered, as we set off again. 'Since his return from Scotland he has been passing strange. Everyone in the house has felt the brunt of his humours.'

'Certainly, to write what he does he must be contrary,' mused Henry. 'A writer's brain swells up, I dare say, from the strain it is put to. And it must overheat all the more in this season.'

He pressed me close and smiled down upon me. 'The heat lends you a becoming pallor, Sarah. And it drives him mad. Well, his renown may be envied. But I consider myself fortunate all the same to be a mere man of the law. There is nothing to heat a man in the law.'

Fearing Mr Hazlitt coming up behind us like a wild beast tracking its prey, I was unable to return Henry's looks of affection, though they were what I had longed most ardent to receive when we started out. I drew apart and smartened my step. Now I could only wish dear that he would leave me and vanish safe from the stares of our stalker into the multitude. For myself, I wished to gain the safety of Southampton Buildings and my chamber.

On turning into the Strand, I made to hurry away on a pretext of being wanted at home and remarked that he might go at his own pace as he liked. He was not inclined always to be so gallant, but on this occasion Henry protested that he had no wish to cut short our stroll and insisted on keeping my company as far as the very door.

'I own I am in a mood to take you as far as Land's End itself, as you are such an agreeable little companion,' he whispered with a laugh.

It made me melancholy that the one time I could not wish it he was seeking to detain me.

'But I see you only want to be rid of me, you impatient girl. Next time, however, I shall insist on taking you further. You must rest and make sure to be able for it.'

'You have my word, sir,' I said with a lightness that was feigned.

Once inside I savoured but for a moment the relief of having delivered us both from the danger and at once ran straight up to the parlour. For, the instant I felt myself safe, I was conscious that I had quit my dear Henry, and was longing to see him again, and eager to spy a last glimpse of him as he turned into Staple Inn. There to my view, sure enough, through the parlour window was his tall slender figure, restoring to his head the hat that he had doffed to me in farewell. And making good headway behind, at half a run so as to catch him up, I saw the shabby, loping and fierce figure of Mr Hazlitt. I dropped to the boards and wept.

41

My brother had the whole tale to tell by supper-time.
How Bill Hazlitt ran amok in the gardens of the Inns,
shouting Mr Tompkins' name, now for a villain, now
for a witness, and pouring out his defamations of me all
the while to the gentlemen he met with on the paths.
Seizing at last upon Mr Tompkins, he sought an
interview. It was granted. Well, I suppose a gentleman
must talk to anyone if it will stay his being called out for
a dupe in public. Cajah observed them as they sat in the
Serjeant's inn, deep in conversation for two hours or
more over tankards of ale.

This act of treachery, I soon saw, was not sufficient to
soothe the desire for vengeance of the rejected lover.
For days and nights together he haunted the inns and
taverns and coffee-houses from the decent to the most
squalid, waylaying strangers and acquaintances alike to
publicise his hurt and my loathsome character. He was
to be observed clutching this man by his neckcloth, that
one by his wrist, when they were not inclined to listen.
It was not the conduct of a gentleman but that was of
small matter to them. After all, I am but a servant-girl
and it is little cause for surprise when a servant-girl is
shown up for a drab.

I saw I had nothing left to save, excepting a certain

person's last shred of belief in me. At the end of a week, I curled my hair with papers and put on my white short-sleeved gown which, though it is my best, I had never thought would do for my wedding dress. When nobody was watching I slipped out and down Chancery-lane and knocked at Took's Court.

The servant admitted me, free and easy as you please, but wearing a brazen smirk that let me know she had some news of me. She kept the bottom of the stairs as I mounted. I knew she intended to play the Betsy and eavesdrop if she could. Well, now I was grist to everyone's mill and had no entitlement to indignation at whatever she or any of them chose to do or to think of me.

I had the impression that the room appeared more staled and worn and drear than when I last had seen it. Henry stood at a small distance by the tumbled bed. He looked so handsome, any girl's heart must have con-tracted to see him, and be joyful that he might be hers. But my courage near crumpled at the sight of his twisted smile. There was no tincture of pleasure or affection to be remarked in it.

'I had not thought to see you,' he said. 'Though indeed I have heard a deal of you. As much as any man could wish to hear.'

'I beg you, sir, do not believe it,' I answered.

'Oh? It is not true, then? Not a word? You are a good girl, who never sat on a man's lap or twined yourself about him? He is mad, you will say. I suppose that is to be your defence. It may be the fault of my lawyer's mind, but I am sure it must be a wonder to anyone why even a madman should think up such lies.'

Dropping my shawl to the floor I revealed my arms that he once admired. I had believed myself to be quite cool from my resolve, but now tears welled into my eyes as I stood before him. I went to him and reached up and brought his head to my front. 'Take me,' I whispered. 'Take me and you shall know that I was good.'

He stood off, though he wore a pallor I well knew as he inspected me.

'You are a pretty thing,' he said in a low thick tone. He wore an expression on his face that had less sweets in it than bitters. 'I have always thought it. I have, you know, been fond of you.'

'Take me,' I pleaded, though the words were caught with sobs.

But he must have made them out, for of a sudden he stepped up and gripped me fast and crushed his mouth on mine. Pulling me quite rough on to the dank-smelling bed, he drew up my petticoats, and very quick it was done. It was not what I ever expected nor hoped for when I was a maid. I knew it as a blow, or a jag, from a blunt though necessary instrument. But as a consequence the white gown was spotted red, and the grey counterpane too, when he looked. And that was as much as I wished for.

'Well, you were not ruined before. Though now you are.' He made a rueful grimace.

'Only by you, sir,' I said, 'so I cannot but be glad, and don't care that I am ruined.'

He was grown a little more gentle by this time and damped my gown with a cloth so that the stains might be more easy washed away. While he combed his hair to his satisfaction in the mirror with a cold and private look, I did up my slackened clothes. I am sure I presented no very pretty picture at that task. Then he said he had to go out and took my shawl from the floor where it had fallen and handed it to me as a means of my dismissal. We descended the stairs across the servant's gaze, and into the glare of the street in silence. He parted from me on Chancery-lane.

238

'Come on Thursday,' he instructed. 'You shall find me at home.'

He did not wait for an assent but turned on his heel and walked brisk away. I knew that, when Thursday came, I would be knocking at Took's Court.

42

To be ruined in the common way is grief enough. But a fat stomach can be any girl's misfortune. Even great ladies are said to have fallen by that wayside – and you can be sure they always will while there are men left in the world. But if it is hushed up and her family keeps her in the house, a girl might keep her shame to herself and only has to endure it in private. I must suffer my shame in public.

Mr Hazlitt stole upon me like the eclipse and, as he withdrew, blighted my life with his inky darkness. He has called his book *Liber Amoris*. That means 'the book of love'. I wish I might laugh like Cajah at Hazlitt's views on that subject and at the comedy of his conduct which he describes in it, for the base of it is that he knows no love but self-love. He believes himself to be tragical and is no more than comical. But neither can the book be comical to me, since the degenerate creature in it who treats so bad the heroic and suffering Hazlitt is given my name – and it lives in the world, just as I do, and gets about a great deal more.

Can old Mr Roscoe still think me an excellent girl? Mr Hazlitt is vindictive enough to be happy if he should not. And that other gentleman in Liverpool, old Mr Tompkins, must be near as glad as is the author of my notoriety. He is armed now with an excellent cause to dissuade his son from the taking on of the fresh burden. And must be grateful indeed to Mr Hazlitt for getting them all off love's barbed hook. Mr Hazlitt well knows what shame is. More than once he discoursed to me on how it is the fear of it that keeps us straight. I dare say he will give a book over to the subject one of these days, but he will not tell in it how he dealt it to me.

Not let about any more, for fear of showing myself to the gentlemen, I keep my room and let fall my needle from the stitching of small clothes as I conjure up fancies of a world without books. For I despise them and think they were better never to be invented. What are they but instruments writers use to dupe us? On account of them, we have no knowledge of our own, nor way of our own for seeing the world. It is the writers who dazzle us by telling us what we are like, and what we should be like. I know now that they write nothing but lies. And on account of them there is no more innocence in the world, nor free conduct, nor any more independence.